Wife Extraordinaire Returns

Also by Kiki Swinson

Playing Dirty
Notorious
Wifey
I'm Still Wifey
Life After Wifey
Still Wifey Material
A Sticky Situation
The Candy Shop
Wife Extraordinaire
Wife Extraordinaire Returns

Anthologies

Sleeping with the Enemy (with Wahida Clark)
Heist (with De'nesha Diamond)
Lifestyles of the Rich and Shameless (with Noire)
A Gangster and a Gentleman
(with De'nesha Diamond)
Most Wanted (with Nikki Turner)
Still Candy Shopping (with Amaleka McCall)
Fistful of Benjamins (with De'nesha Diamond)

Published by Kensington Publishing Corp.

Wife
Extraordinaire
Returns

KIKI
SWINSON

Kensington Publishing Corp.
http://www.kensingtonbooks.com

DAFINA BOOKS are published by

Kensington Publishing Corp.
850 Third Avenue
New York, NY 10022

All Kensington Titles, Imprints, and Distributed Lines are
available at special quantity discounts for bulk purchases for
sales promotions, premiums, fund-raising, and educational
or institutional use. Special book excerpts or customized
printings can also be created to fit specific needs. For details,
write or phone the office of the Kensington special sales
manager: Kensington Publishing Corp., 850 Third Avenue,
New York, NY 10022, attn: Special Sales Department, Phone:
1-800-221-2647.

Dafina and the Dafina logo Reg. U.S. Pat. & TM Off.

ISBN-13: 978-0-7582-9381-7
ISBN-10: 0-7582-9381-X

First Dafina Mass Market Edition: September 2014

10 9 8 7 6 5 4 3

Printed in the United States of America

Wife
Extraordinaire
Returns

1

Trice

"Leon! No! Please stop!" I screamed, feeling blood rushing to my face.

"Motherfucker! You thought I was gonna let you fuck my wife and take yours back and live happily ever after?!" Leon yelled as he waved the gun at Troy.

Troy looked like a man possessed. His eyes were bloodshot, and his fists were curled tightly.

"Fuck you, nigga! I didn't fuck that skank Charlene! But you wasted no time fucking my wife!" Troy growled as he lunged at Leon. I ran to come between them. I didn't want them to fight over me. Just as I came toward Troy, I stopped in my tracks.

BAM! BAM! I heard the shots so loudly I didn't even feel any pain.

I could feel myself screaming, but amazingly, I

couldn't hear myself. Next, I felt a hot burning sensation envelop my body.

BAM! BAM! Two more shots and everything in my world went black.

I jumped out of my sleep covered in sweat. I swallowed hard and looked over at Troy. He was sleeping soundly as usual. I guess it was easy for him, since he wasn't the one who'd almost died. I had been severely shot and almost died. The hospital staff saved my life when Troy thought the lifeless body covered with a white sheet belonged to me. He didn't know it, but I had been taken out of that operating room long before the other person had been brought in. God rest her soul.

Luckily for me, two shots went straight through—one in my shoulder, the other in my arm. It was the third shot that had done me damage. As a result, I had my spleen removed. But what hurt most were the infidelities that transpired between all of us. I don't remember much about that night, except that Troy had come over to the hotel I was hiding out in. Unfortunately, Leon came as well. Things escalated when Troy realized that during the spouse trade, Leon and I had had sex. As it turned out, it wasn't my fault things with Leon and I had gone to that level.

Leon's wife, Charlene, had convinced me that she had had sex with my husband first. She had said some very cruel things to me over the phone, and I was crushed to my core. When she told me Troy had just finished eating her out and that he was *indisposed*, as she put it, I was devastated beyond belief.

Out of revenge and hurt, I slept with Leon. I had no idea the feelings would grow into what we did. So, when he got sentenced to all that time, I was hurt.

It had been seven months since my husband, Troy, and I had participated in the hit reality show *Trading Spouses*. It had also been seven months since that fucking show ruined our lives and the lives of Troy's best friend, Leon, and his wife, Charlene.

The guys had been childhood buddies and best friends almost all of their lives. They had done everything together growing up, but all of that changed. When we'd agreed to trade spouses for one week for ten thousand dollars, none of us knew it wouldn't be worth it in the end. Because Charlene disconnected the cameras in our house, we were sanctioned and no one was paid one red cent. The TV execs did pay for my medical bills, but aside from that, we didn't get shit.

Troy and I tried to repair our marriage in the aftermath of it all. But in my eyes, it was over. When I found out I was pregnant, I decided it would probably be best for me to hold on to someone for the baby's sake . . . rather than becoming a statistic.

Troy was the closest thing.

I looked around my bedroom, and a cold feeling came over me just thinking about the shit that had happened. I touched my very pregnant belly and felt my baby move inside of me. I closed my eyes and sighed. *Baby* was the operative word . . . because the father was an issue. Although Troy believed it was his baby, I thought for sure I knew differently.

"Trice? You okay, baby?" Troy asked, rousing from his sleep. I kept my back to him and closed my eyes.

"I'm fine. Just another nightmare," I said without looking at him.

Troy reached out and rubbed his hands over my back. His touch made me feel dirty and partly guilty. I had been thinking about Leon in that moment.

"How's my little bun in the oven doing?" Troy asked, still rubbing my back.

"Fine. The baby is fine," I replied, a little annoyed. I stood up swiftly and grabbed my robe from the end of our bed. I rolled my eyes as I left the room. I shuddered at Troy being all mushy and loving. He had been nothing but good to me since the entire incident with Leon. But I couldn't get my feelings to change toward him for anything. Somewhere in the back of my

4

mind, I blamed Troy for everything that had happened.

I was still convinced he'd slept with Charlene. The producers of the show couldn't help me disprove it. And since that dumb bitch Charlene had disconnected the camera wires, that didn't do shit for my suspicions. Why else would she have disconnected the cameras if they weren't fucking?

I knew all about how grimy Charlene was from Leon. He told me how she was a lazy hood rat that barely took care of their son, and she never did any of the cleaning around the house. She was uneducated, and all she did was hustle the welfare system to make extra money. In other words, Charlene was a bum bitch.

Leon had assured me repeatedly that I had way more class than Charlene. He had also aired Troy's dirty laundry by telling me that Troy had thought about cheating on me once. Troy had gotten so close that he and the girl were naked before he backed out of it. Leon also told me that Troy complained that I didn't fuck him enough or suck his dick at all. Wasn't that some bullshit?

It was just like Troy to tell half the fucking story. I knew Leon wasn't making shit up because it was true. I refused to suck Troy's dick, and I also rationed out the pussy. I loved Troy for how good he was as a provider and person, but his dick game was whack. His dick was so skinny and short that most times I couldn't even feel it. It was like getting fucked by a baby.

When Troy and I dated, I tried to ignore the horrible sex by keeping my eye on the prize. The prize was having a house, nice car, nice things, and of course, security. I thought I could just look past the fact that his sex was horrendous and fall in love with everything else, like Troy's personality. He had the ability to provide the fairy-tale life we had.

Well, after we got married, I just couldn't do it. I tried and tried. Troy would beg for sex, and sometimes I would just give in for argument's sake. Most times, I would lie there praying for it to be over ... all five minutes of it. I mean, he even had the nerve to be a fucking two-minute brother with a small dick.

I tried buying sex toys and that worked for a while, but sometimes I longed for some good ol' righteous hard dick. I wanted and needed some real skin-to-skin contact, not that plastic feeling from my toys. I wanted a man to use his God-given gift to dig my back out. Unfortunately for Troy, during the spouse trade, that's exactly what happened. Leon's dick was huge and oh so good. And during our lovemaking, I had an orgasm for the first time in ten years. Leon had fucked me in several different positions that I never dared to try with Troy. It was frustrating as hell to always have Troy's little dick fall out of my pussy. I couldn't imagine how frustrated I would get trying anything other than our traditional missionary position. Hell, even when we did the doggie position, his little dick would constantly slip out.

But Leon was different. He had me hooked, although I was fighting the reality of what he had done to me. I tried to put Leon and his sex out of my mind, but between feeling vulnerable after finding out that Troy had the nerve to cheat on me with Charlene and having Leon comfort me with that beautiful piece of meat, I was all in. I was head over heels for Leon so fast that I had amazed even myself. I was ready to walk away from my marriage and even live a more modest life. Leon wasn't as successful and didn't have as much as Troy, but the sex had me ready to throw it all away—the house, the cars, the fat bank account, and everything Troy did for me.

But I knew Troy . . . and he wouldn't let go that easily.

I shook off the thoughts of Leon and his wonderful dick as I walked out of the bedroom and headed downstairs. It was still dark outside. I shuffled my swollen feet into the kitchen and poured a glass of milk. I quietly lifted a metal canister off the top of the refrigerator and retrieved the secret cell phone I had purchased. I slid it into my robe pocket and sat down with my glass of milk. I didn't hear any footsteps coming from upstairs, which probably meant Troy had scratched his balls and went right back to sleep.

I looked around, ensuring I was careful. I took out the phone and powered it up. My heart raced feverishly as the missed calls began appearing on the phone.

"Damn," I cursed under my breath. They were all missed calls from the prison facility where Leon was housed. I had gotten the phone just to have secret communications with him. It was foul, I know, but I couldn't help it.

I was reading through all of the missed calls, trying to put together the last time Leon called me. I was so engrossed scrolling through the numbers and lost in thought that I didn't hear Troy enter the kitchen.

"Whatcha got there?" Troy asked, smiling from the doorway.

"Oh shit!" I exclaimed, dropping the phone into my lap. "You scared the shit out of me, Troy! What're you trying to do, make me go into labor early? And why in the hell are you sneaking up on me?!" I gasped, placing my hand over my chest.

He had caught me red-handed, but I had recovered fast.

"Damn, Trice, calm down. I just wanted to make sure you were okay. You got out of bed so abruptly," Troy replied, looking at me strangely as he walked toward the table where I was sitting.

"Well, make some noise next time. I mean, it's like you are always lurking in the shadows somewhere," I said, making sure the phone went into the pocket of my robe.

"Were you reading something?" Troy probed, standing over me.

"No, I wasn't. I happened to be saying my daily prayer," I lied. I got up from the table so hard the kitchen chair went slamming to the floor. "I didn't know you worked for the FBI now!" I snapped, stomping out of the kitchen. I had to get away from his ass fast.

"Damn, I can't wait for your moody ass to have that baby. You treat me like shit on a daily!" I heard Troy yelling at my back.

"Oh, shut the fuck up," I mumbled in response.

I needed to get the fuck out of the house so I could accept the twelve o'clock call from Leon. Speaking to him was the only thing that would make me feel better right now.

2

Charlene

I was dead-dog tired when I left the Glass Slipper strip club, my new place of employment. I couldn't get behind the wheel of my car and head home fast enough. I hadn't even bothered to take off the thick layer of makeup I wore during my act. Plus, my hair was still pulled back in a stubby ponytail from where I took off my costume wig. I didn't have time to do shit. My legs ached, my back was sore, and I felt as if I had the finger-prints of every man in Virginia Beach all over my ass.

I was longing for a hot shower to get all the stink and grime from the dirty niggas in the club off me. I was also dying to get into my bed for a long, well-deserved sleep. Whenever I felt this terrible after a night at the club, I found myself being very pissed off that I even had to go back to stripping.

It was all thanks to my stupid-ass husband, Leon, who got his dumb ass locked up for trying to kill his best friend, Troy, and accidentally shooting Trice, Troy's wife. Imagine that, I was reduced to working the pole because my husband was trying to fight for another man's wife. Now that was some crazy shit!

The night Leon went gun happy, I had arrived at the scene of the incident shortly after it had gone down. I couldn't believe my eyes when I saw the police bringing Leon out in handcuffs and the EMTs rushing Trice out on a stretcher. Honestly, seeing that snobby bitch on a stretcher, I secretly wished that her ass was dead. She had both men, her husband and mine, going crazy over her. Yet, neither one of them had any respect for me.

Troy had cursed me out and treated me like shit when he had returned me to Leon. When I got back home, Leon told me he wasn't fucking with me and he didn't want me anymore. It hurt a lot to think I couldn't get Troy to fuck me during the spouse trade. But it hurt even more to know it was so easy for Trice to get Leon to want her.

Still, after all of his rejections and disrespect, I showed up to all of Leon's court dates. At first, it was to mock him and hope they put his ass under the jail. But then seeing him so broken down, I decided to show up to support him. I knew it was dumb, but it was really who I was inside, contrary to popular belief that I was a heartless bitch.

Leon had decided to give up on going to trial and he pled guilty to involuntary manslaughter. He got a few years knocked off his sentence in exchange for the plea. But he was sentenced to seven to ten years in prison. Of course, this nigga was crying the *baby, baby, I love you so much* song after he found out how long he got.

He wasn't saying that shit when he was betraying me by chasing behind Trice after we all participated in the show *Trading Spouses*. This dude had the nerve to fall in love with Trice after one week! *Who in the hell falls in love after one week?!* I had been with his trifling, cheating, dirty-dick ass for seven years, and after seven days with her, he was trying to wife her up and give me my fucking walking papers.

At first, I was like, fuck you, nigga, but after he got knocked for the shooting incident and Troy got back with Trice, I decided I would try—and that's *try* with a big T-R-Y—to stick by Leon through his bid.

Trying was trying my fucking nerves right about now. Everything was a constant struggle without Leon's income and support. I had no skills, no education, and no regular job. I had to even beg for my gig back at the club, because I had gained weight and sported some stretch marks on my thighs and stomach after I gave birth to my son. Leon had screwed up my life big-time!

He left nothing but six hundred dollars in the bank account when he got locked up, and we never got the ten thousand dollars from the show. The producers made up some bullshit story about me disconnecting cameras in Troy and Trice's house, which caused all four of us to forfeit the money. I almost got arrested for kicking the producer's ass when she told me that bullshit. I know for sure I put those wires back correctly, and those motherfuckers knew I did too.

Anyway, I had to turn back to the club to feed my son and keep a roof over our heads. Not to mention, like a fucking dummy, I was putting money on Leon's books at the prison. For some reason, as much as I hated what happened with Trice and Leon and all the foul shit Leon had told Troy about me being a lazy, Section 8, ghetto hood rat, I still loved Leon and wanted our relationship to work out. I wasn't sure if it was because I felt a sense of competition with Trice and wanted to prove to that bitch that I could keep my husband or if it was that I was dick-whipped by Leon and just didn't want to let that shit go.

It was no secret around Norfolk that Leon had an Adonis dick. He had cheated on me many times, so a lot of females knew how good his shit was. I was proud to say that the dick belonged to me even though I knew I was sharing it with a lot of his side hoes. I couldn't tell anyone that I stuck by Leon because his dick was good, so I saved face by telling all my friends that I stuck by Leon for the sake of our son. That was a lie. Shit, everybody in Norfolk had kids growing up without fathers. What the fuck would be the difference? For me, the difference was simple—I didn't want to look like a dumb bitch in front of my friends. I needed my dignity to stay intact.

Leon's thing with Trice made me realize one thing—I was still a woman with emotions and feelings. As many bitches as Leon had fucked throughout the Norfolk area, he had never fallen in love or done anything stupid like trying to shoot a bitch's husband. I don't know what got into his stupid ass. That bitch's pussy couldn't be as good as my shit. But that's the thing that hurt the most. The bastard lost his mind over another bitch. That was the insult I had to live with for the rest of my life . . . and I didn't like that shit, didn't like it at all.

I put my key into the door of my economy apartment and had never been so glad to be home. As soon as I stepped inside, I heard the phone ringing. I threw my bag down and raced to the small kitchen. I grabbed the cordless phone off the cradle and pressed the TALK button.

"Hello," I huffed into the receiver.

"Yo! Why I been calling all morning and I can't get your ass?" Leon barked into the phone. I rolled my eyes and pulled the phone from my ear while he yelled.

"I had to work, nigga! What do you think? I had to do two private champagne room stints in order to make these fucking bills this month. My last one ran over!" I screamed at his ass. He had some fucking nerve!

"What them niggas do to you in them private parties?" Leon asked, his tone accusatory as hell. I rolled my eyes and clenched my fists. He had to be kidding me with these questions.

"Look, you know our agreement on this shit, Leon. Don't fucking ask and I won't fucking tell!" I barked. "As long as I put money on your damn books and come to see you and take care of your motherfucking son, we shouldn't have any problems. Remember, I didn't put you in prison!" I could feel the veins in my neck pulsing. I was ready to hang up on this nigga for real. I was too damn tired for the bullshit.

"You right, Charlene. You right," Leon said calmly, quickly changing his tone. "Are you coming on the visit tomorrow?" he asked.

I rolled my eyes and flopped down in one of the mismatched kitchen chairs. I wanted to cry or kill myself realizing how low I had sunk because of this motherfucker. Small apartment, small kitchen, mismatched chairs. Shit, I deserved better.

"I have to take LJ to his baseball game if it don't rain, so I'm not sure," I said dryly. What I really wanted to say was, *Bitch, if you were here to take your son to his games, I wouldn't have to!*

"Well, when am I gonna see you, then?" Leon

asked like a sad puppy. I twisted my lips because he was getting to me once again. I wanted to kick my own ass. This asshole had no power over me, but here I was feeling bad for this nigga once again.

"I don't know, Leon. I'm gonna get up there as soon as I can. I mean, if I miss one Saturday, it's not going to kill you, is it?" I asked, trying real hard to soften my tone.

"Nah, but you can't come to the Tuesday visits, so I was just asking to make sure I won't be sitting around like a lame nigga waiting for a visit that ain't gonna happen."

"A'ight. Well, don't expect to see me, then. I'll come on the next visit," I told him. Shit, what did he want me to say? Bad enough I was doing everything on my own; now he wanted to make fucking demands. I couldn't care less if he was sitting around waiting on a visit . . . last I checked, his ass didn't have shit else to do!

"That's real fucked up, Charlene, but I understand. I'll holla," Leon said in a real nasty tone.

I opened my mouth to blast his ass, but he hung up on me. I had to look at the phone a couple of times before I could believe his audacity.

"The nerve of this bitch-ass nigga!" I yelled. I threw the phone down and headed to my bed. I was fucking sick and tired. Real sick and tired of the bullshit!

3

Troy

Trice had just left me standing in the kitchen looking and feeling like a total fool. I didn't know how much more of her blatant disrespect I could take. It hadn't been the same since we did the show *Trading Spouses*, and the shooting incident that occurred definitely put a real strain on our marriage. I think Trice still blamed me for everything that happened, especially for the fact that she ended up clinging to life in the hospital.

It had been my idea to do the show in the first place, and Leon went along with it. He and I had been best friends since childhood, and up until then we'd trusted each other with our lives. When I saw the advertisement for the show, it sounded appealing as hell. I thought, shit, he wanted a break from his wife, Charlene, and I wanted a break from Trice's nagging, no-sex-having ass. On top of that, both families would get ten thousand dollars. Overall, it was supposed to be a great deal: ten grand and a break from our wives.

When Leon and I pitched the idea to our wives, Trice was the only one hesitant about doing it. Charlene's money-hungry ass was down from the word go. When I finally convinced Trice that it was going to be a walk in the park, especially since she wasn't getting traded to a complete stranger, she finally agreed. It was one week—seven days. I thought there wasn't much that could happen in seven short days. Shit, I was sadly mistaken. As it turned out, *Trading Spouses* became the worst mistake of my life.

From day one, I was in over my head. The differences between Trice and Charlene were like comparing a Ruth's Chris steak to a McDonald's Happy Meal. Charlene was not as beautiful as Trice. She was the color of bad coffee beans, wore tons of weave, and had a thick ass and hips, while Trice had a butterscotch complexion, naturally curly, long hair, and a model's perfect ass. Additionally, Charlene was ghetto as hell and Trice was sophisticated and refined.

But I doomed myself. Regardless of how many times Leon had told me about how provocative Charlene was and how top rank her pussy was, I thought this would be easy money. I was naïve. From the beginning, my mind was thinking about Leon's words on the terrific head that Charlene gave. Looking at her lips, I could easily believe that. Then seeing her strutting around bare-ass naked, my imagination ran wild with thoughts of skull fucking her and sticking my dick deep down her throat. And who could blame me? Trice hardly ever gave me sex.

But I prevailed, I was the stronger man, although Charlene tried to tempt me with that phat ass she had. Somehow I resisted her numerous attempts to get me to sleep with her. But I found out that conniving, no-good bitch had devised a plan to sabotage my marriage. Unbeknownst to me, she had told Trice that I had fucked her and that I didn't want to be with Trice any longer. And my stupid, ignorant-ass wife believed that shit. Trice took that bit of information and ran with it. Or I should say her dumb ass ran into the comforting arms of my so-called friend, Leon. I'm sure one thing led to another.

The sad thing is Trice never told me this. First, I figured the shit out myself from Leon's crazy ass trying to kill me over my wife. And no motherfucker would do that for a woman he hadn't slept with. Second, when he made his plea bargain in court, he had to state why Trice was shot. He told the judge that Trice wasn't the person he was trying to shoot. It was my life he was trying to take, and to make matters worse, this nigga had the audacity to say he had fallen in love with Trice.

For a nigga who had fucked half the bitches in Norfolk, I knew then he had the pussy, and evidently, Trice had laid the shit on him real decent. So, he was pussy-whipped. And that's why I hope his ass dies in prison.

Unfortunately for me, like Trice, I couldn't get that dreaded night out of my head. That was a fucked-up night. First, Trice told me she was leaving me for that motherfucker. Then, Charlene called me and said Trice was hiding out at a hotel waiting for Leon. I did what every real man would do. I took action and went to reclaim my wife. As it turned out, Leon was ready to fight for Trice as well. And not just fight—this stupid motherfucker was ready to kill me for my wife. That nigga must've smoked some dope before he ran up on me.

He pulled a gun on me and when we got to fighting, accidental discharges hit Trice. Not once, but three times. Thank God she was still alive. I thought the shooting would change the way she felt about me. I was there every hour of the day while she recovered. We found out while she was in the hospital that she was in the very early stages of a pregnancy. By the grace of God, we were fortunate she didn't lose the baby. A real miracle.

I have wanted a baby for years, but with the few and far between sex sessions Trice and I had, she had never gotten pregnant. I was over the moon to find out she was pregnant, and when we later found out at the sonogram that the baby was a girl, it made it more of a blessing.

The pregnancy had been hard on Trice, especially since she had some residual medical issues from the shooting. I tried to understand her raging hormones and feelings, but I am human too. Trice literally walked around angry with me all the fucking time. Many days when I got home from work, she wasn't there. When I tried calling her, she ignored my calls and let her phone go to voice mail.

It seemed like every Tuesday she left before I went to work and wasn't there when I returned home. If I dared to ask her where she had been, she would scream at me as if I were a damn child. My patience was short. I was tired of trying to be the good guy and she insisted on being the bitch.

I gave her back rubs and foot massages, waited on her ungrateful ass hand and foot when I was home, and nothing was ever good enough. Forget about the great pregnancy sex I hear so many men talk so much about. My stupid ass wouldn't know anything about that shit. Trice was back to her old ways of keeping the pussy under lock and key from me. It was a sad case. Maybe I was the sad case. But I was locked in now . . . in other words, no way was I going anywhere with my baby coming.

I stood in the kitchen dumbfounded as she stormed out as if I had done something to her, just because I asked her what she was reading. Damn, it was small talk! I looked around and decided to pack my own lunch for work. Another thing Trice wasn't doing anymore.

It was a sad situation in my household, and I couldn't help but feel it was all my fault. I climbed back up the stairs to our bedroom to get dressed for work, and I heard Trice inside our room crying. I stood by the door for a minute and then I walked in.

"Trice? What's wrong, baby?" I asked, trying to use my best patient tone.

"Nothing. You wouldn't understand," she replied, wiping tears from her face. That answer had me baffled.

"Understand what? Try talking to me and maybe I will understand," I told her. I didn't know what else to say. "Is it the baby? Your hormones? Did something happen?" I rambled off questions like I was a therapist.

"I don't want to talk about it, Troy! I just want you to give me some space. I know you want to be the good husband, but I am still not mentally strong," Trice said through tears.

I went to hug her and she pushed me away. I pulled my hands back and lifted them in front of me in surrender. There was nothing I could do to make my wife happy anymore. Sometimes I couldn't help but feel as if she still wanted to

be with Leon. I stormed into our master bathroom and slammed the door. I punched at the
air out of frustration. My imagination was getting the best of me, because something in my gut
was telling me that my wife mentally and emotionally belonged to another man.

*The same motherfucker who damn near put her six
feet under.*

What kind of shit was that?

4

Leon

Niggas in line for the phone were looking at me like I was crazy. I gave a screwface to them cats. "What . . . y'all ain't never hang up on a bitch before?" I snarled.

I wasn't one of those scared-ass niggas that a bitch thought was gonna be kissing her ass because I was locked up. The only reason I convinced Charlene I still wanted to be with her ass after that fucking *Trading Spouses* shit was because I needed her as a backup plan. When I got knocked, I told her all the shit she wanted to hear—that I was sorry, that I had made a mistake, that Trice was just another piece of ass, that I needed her and there was no one else like her.

Charlene fell for that shit hook, line, and sinker. I told her if she did this bid with me, when I got out early on good behavior, we would leave Norfolk and put the past behind us. Oh, I was leaving Norfolk, but I wasn't taking bird-ass Charlene with me.

There was one thing I had to thank Charlene for: running her stupid-ass mouth to cause problems between Trice and Troy. That gave me the opportunity to swoop in, give Trice some of this good dick, and get her to be with me.

After finding out that Charlene had answered Troy's phone and told Trice she and Troy had just finished fucking, I was furious. I knew it was a lie, but that conniving bitch did me a huge favor. She also told Trice that Troy didn't want to be with her and after the trade he would be leaving her. I don't think I had ever seen a woman more devastated than I saw Trice that night. She cried in my arms for hours.

I realized real fast that Trice was more my type than Charlene could ever be. Trice was reserved, classy, and pretty, and I knew a lot of niggas hadn't run through her pussy like they had Charlene's. Trice was also interested in the same things I was, from sports and working out to seeing movies on the first night they were released. She had even gone with me on my daily morning run a couple of times.

Man, I couldn't get Charlene to run, work out,

or sit and watch a football or basketball game with me for shit. And forget going to a good crime-thriller movie with her and discussing it afterward. The trick monster couldn't catch on to plot twists or anything if they bit her in the ass. She was a true airhead and hood rat. Granted, I had cheated on her a few times, but that was because she never kept my interest. Her sex was great, that was a fact, but there was so much more to me than just sex.

I got back to my cell and sat on my bunk. My cellmate, Kenny, came in shortly after me.

"Yo, nigga, I heard you was banging the jack on a chick today," Kenny said.

I wasn't in the mood for his prison grapevine chitchat today. "Why niggas talk so much?" I snapped.

"Niggas are like bitches up in this camp, you know that shit. What's going on, man? Drama out in the world?" Kenny continued.

"Something like that," I answered.

Kenny started laughing hysterically.

"What's so funny?" I asked, sitting up and eye-screwing him.

"You the only dude I know got two chicks coming to see you on those visits and you still not satisfied. It's just funny to me," Kenny replied, still chuckling.

I lightened my mood at what he said. He was right. I was known as a pimp around the cellblock. I had Trice and Charlene alternating visits and both of them putting money on my books. Trice came to the Tuesday visit and Charlene came on Saturday. I was getting tired of seeing Charlene, and with Trice getting bigger with my baby inside of her, I wanted to see her more often. I knew getting in an argument with Charlene would make her ass stay home on Saturday. Plus, making her put my son into Little League eliminated a lot of visit days too.

"I'm the man, so I have to work my magic," I said, and we both busted out laughing.

"So which one is coming this Saturday, yellow mellow or chocolate chip?" Kenny joked some more.

"You a clown, nigga. The one I want to see is my high-yellow honey. I can't wait to get out so I can cut that bitch Charlene off altogether," I told him.

"Well, damn, ain't Charlene the one riding this bid with you while the other chick is laying up in her cozy little crib and playing house with her husband? That bitch is probably fucking that nigga every night so he can feed your unborn baby some of his daddy juices," Kenny commented.

His words made me instantly hot inside. I could actually picture Trice and Troy fucking and him rubbing her pregnant belly with my baby inside. I felt possessed. I jumped up and grabbed Kenny by the throat.

"Yo! Don't fucking disrespect Trice! I will

have you dead up in this fucking cell," I growled in his face. Kenny was turning red, even though his face was black as coal. "If you ever open your mouth to say anything about my girl again, you won't be getting off this easily," I said, then released him with a shove.

Kenny went reeling back and started coughing, trying to catch his breath. "Nigga, you done fucked with the wrong dude behind these bars. You as good as a dead man," Kenny gasped out.

"Whatever, nigga. You better sleep with one eye open," I told him. I was playing tough, but I knew Kenny had friends behind the walls. I was really going to have to keep my eyes peeled and my guard up.

5

Trice

Two days had passed and I was finally able to speak to Leon on my secret cell phone. He was pissed with me because he'd been trying to reach me, but I put him at ease as usual with updates on the baby. Leon told me he wanted me to come see him today, which was Saturday, and that struck me as strange. I knew he still had Charlene coming up there on Saturday so he could see his son.

Leon assured me Charlene had cursed him out and said she wasn't coming. That was perfect for me. I would be able to see him twice. I could hardly sleep the entire night thinking about seeing Leon. Sometimes I thought I was losing my mind for dissing Troy for a convict, but something inside of me wouldn't let me cut that connection with Leon.

I eased out of bed so Troy wouldn't wake up. I was moving as fast as my pregnant body would allow me without making a lot of noise. I couldn't get dressed fast enough. It was Saturday, and I knew if I didn't get out of the house fast, Troy was going to be asking what we were going to do today. I wasn't trying to hang with his ass at all. Lately, I found myself treating him like shit, because I didn't respect him and I certainly had fallen out of love with him.

I peeked over at him one last time before I crept down the stairs to the front door. I grabbed my car keys off the hook by the door and waddled to my car. The sun hadn't even come up yet. Saturday visits were early, and with the long visitors' processing at the prison, I wanted to be sure I got there early. I pulled out of the driveway and took one last look at the house. I could've sworn I saw the curtains moving, but I shook it off. I knew Troy was knocked out inside.

When I arrived at the prison, I went through the usual identification checks, body searches, and processing. I was led to the visitors' room and waited in anticipation for Leon to come out. Finally, I saw him being led over by the corrections officer. I let a huge Cheshire cat smile spread across my face and stood up. Leon was smiling too. His teeth were gleaming, and his dark skin was still smooth and vibrant despite his being locked up. He had a neatly groomed haircut, and even in a prison jumpsuit, Leon still had more swag than Troy could ever even hope to have.

Leon approached me and gave me a big hug. His chest and arms felt thicker and harder than I remembered them. I knew it was the result of having nothing else to do but lift weights in prison. Of course, the corrections officer wasn't having that kind of physical contact and gave Leon a stern warning.

"Hey, baby girl, how are you and my other baby girl?" Leon asked, still smiling from ear to ear. I blushed. He was so sweet but in a rugged way. Unlike Troy, who was sweet but so damn corny.

"We are doing just fine health-wise. But you know as each day gets closer to my due date, I get more and more nervous. I don't know who she'll look like, and Troy is a lot of things, but he is not stupid," I told Leon.

His face took on a serious expression. "Look, I don't really want to hear about how that nigga is gonna feel when the baby comes," Leon began. "I understand about you staying with him right now, because you don't have no place else to go and I'm locked up . . . but after that baby comes, I'm not gonna have you playing house with Troy and my seed, Trice. You gonna have to find some other arrangement until I can get back in the world and help you."

I just knew I wasn't hearing him correctly. Was he really being demanding to me? He couldn't be serious with the shit he was talking. I looked at him like he'd lost his mind.

"Leon, I love you and all, but I'm not leaving Troy right now or when the baby comes unless he figures things out and kicks me out. This baby, whether she is yours or not, deserves better than a father who is in jail and can't help raise her. I'm sorry to say that I will be with Troy until you are out and about and ready to step in," I kindly informed him.

There was no way I was going to even lead him to believe that I was going to leave my home because of his demands. He was in prison with a lot of years, or did he forget that little nugget of information? Leon rubbed his hands over his face and blew out a frustrated breath. "I'm sorry, but I have to do what is right by the baby. You'll have to put it out of your mind—that's it and that's all," I finished.

"Yeah, a'ight! Whatever!" Leon finally said dejectedly. I could tell he was pissed. He was trying hard to keep his composure with me. I had already seen firsthand how angry and violent he could get. I was still battling with the fact that he'd actually shot me. I had forgiven him and rationalized my forgiveness by blaming my getting shot on Troy for lunging at Leon.

I touched the top of Leon's hand gently and

softened my gaze. "I don't mean to be so blunt about it, but what else do you expect from me? This is not the ideal situation for any of us, especially for a baby who didn't ask to be here," I said.

"Yeah, a'ight. I'm done talking about it. I know, you gotta do what you gotta do. Moving on to other shit, did you put any money in my commissary?"

"Yes, I took some money out of Troy's stash account and put some on your books. I had to do that because Troy just paid all of the bills, and there was no extra cash in our regular account. If he asks me about it, I will tell him I started buying stuff for the baby. He'll go for that excuse," I replied. Leon chuckled a little bit. I looked at him like he was losing his mind.

"What? What's so funny?" I asked.

"I'm just thinking about how foul that shit sounds. Stealing from your husband to hit off the other man's prison commissary," Leon said.

I felt a flash of heat flit through my chest. I guess it was a mixture of embarrassment and anger. Leon was right, but I was doing it out of love for him, so why should he complain. I noticed lately he was always trying to point out things I did for him in comparison to things I did for Troy. I guess it was a pissing match in Leon's eyes.

"Well, it was either that or you have no money.

Look, I came all the way here to see you. Let's stop beefing over bullshit," I told him. Enough was enough.

"You right. I'm sorry. Stand up so I can touch my daughter," Leon instructed. I stood up and he placed his hands on my belly. The baby jumped inside of me and started moving around like crazy. She had never moved around like that when Troy touched me. It was the weirdest thing. I guess even she knew her real father's touch.

6

Charlene

My weave was sweated completely out, and the hair of my Chinese bang was plastered to my forehead by the time I arrived at the prison. I had been running, rushing, and killing myself to get there since I changed my mind about visiting Leon at the last minute. I had just made the last visitor cutoff time. I was usually there for the first visit time.

I shifted my weight from one foot to the next while I waited in the processing line. My feet were killing me and my legs were cold. I had on the things Leon always required me to wear——my come-fuck-me pumps and the shortest miniskirt in my closet, so he could finger my pussy under the table when the COs weren't looking.

"Next!" I heard the processing CO scream out.

I moved to the counter and extended my ID to her. "Leon Bunch," I said. I watched as her fingers pecked the computer keyboard rapidly.

"Who you say again?" the CO asked me, her face crinkled into a frown.

"Leon Bunch," I repeated, furrowing my eyebrows at her as if she were a stupid-ass. She started pecking again, and then she looked at me strangely.

"Miss, I'm sorry, but Mr. Bunch already had a visit today," the CO informed me.

My heart started pumping fast as hell and more sweat broke out on my head. "That's impossible! I'm the only person that visits him and I just got here," I told her with much attitude. "Check your little system again. You must have the wrong Leon Bunch!" I snapped. I was looking at the bitch like she had ten heads and was a fire-breathing dragon. The CO pecked on some more buttons; then she chuckled like I had made a fucking joke. I was gritting on her like I wanted to smack the hell out of her.

"Sorry to inform you that we only have one Leon Bunch in our system. You can look for yourself and check the date of birth while you're at it. Here is his visitor log for this week," the CO replied smugly as she turned the computer monitor so I could see it. She used her index finger to point to the line where Leon's visits were listed. I moved in for a closer look. When I read

Leon's Tuesday and Saturday visitor log, my legs got weak and my knees almost buckled. I was blinking rapidly to keep the tears from falling out of my eyes and to try to save face in front of the CO.

"See, a Trice Davis visited both days, so you can't be the *only* one visiting him," the CO said, putting the emphasis on the word *only* I had used earlier.

I let out a nervous little chuckle and placed my hand over my chest like I was relieved. "Oh, that's just his sister. I thought I would have to get crazy," I laughed, trying to play it off. The room was actually spinning around, and I felt an overwhelming urge to vomit. I didn't know what to do next. Here I was neglecting my son's baseball game, giving up my morning, rushing to the prison, and all along this motherfucker was still seeing that bitch Trice.

"That's what they all say when they find out," the CO said sarcastically, with a look on her face that made me want to just punch the shit out of her.

"So you have to either wait until Tuesday or next Saturday," the CO followed up. "I'm going to have to ask you to move aside so I can process this line of people."

"Can I get a printout of that screen?" I asked her. She looked at me as if I were crazy at first, and then she looked around. She used her mouse to click something. Then she slid the paper to me.

"I'm not supposed to do this, but I'm a woman too. I know how it feels to be lied to when you bust your ass to be there for these niggas while they are locked up," the CO whispered.

I couldn't say anything to her, because she was absolutely right. I was just happy she believed in sisterhood.

"Next!" the CO called out, giving me the eye to move along.

I stumbled to the left. I felt as if my world was off-kilter. My insides were boiling, and I didn't know if I was more mad or hurt. I got back on the shuttle bus that took visitors to the main gate and parking lot. I rushed to my car, and once I was inside, I broke down crying. I kept reading the paper over and over again. Seeing that bitch's name made me crazy. I slammed my hands on the steering wheel so hard that the skin on my knuckles busted. If it were Trice's face, she would've been beaten bloody.

"You motherfucker! I'm out here struggling and busting my ass. Letting men feel up my pussy and squeeze my breasts for you and this is the thanks I get? I hate you, Leon! I fucking hate you, you son of a bitch!" I screamed at the top of my lungs as if Leon could somehow hear me.

I was so enraged that I didn't even realize I had also broken four of my newly done nails and my fingertips were bleeding. My heart hadn't ached this badly since the first time I learned this lying, cheating-ass nigga was fucking another bitch on the side.

We had been together for a year, and I was six months pregnant with our son, when this young chick from around my way came to my house to confront me about her relationship with Leon. She had knocked on my door, and when I answered, she immediately sucker punched me in the face and caught me off guard. My nose had gushed blood, and by the time Leon had gotten to the door, the girl's friends had pulled her back down the steps.

While I tried to get the bleeding under control with paper towels, I could hear the girl outside my house yelling about how she had been fucking Leon for the past six months and that every time I kissed Leon, I was tasting her pussy. Then she said she knew I was having a baby boy, because Leon had told her I went to my sonogram appointment alone since he didn't believe the baby was his. The girl also knew my due date and told me where I had been the night before.

I was floored. But that's how I knew the girl wasn't lying about fucking with Leon. How else would she know Leon had ditched me and made me go to the sonogram appointment alone? How else would she have known I was with my girlfriends the night before and my due date?

That bitch knew so much information she could tell me my last fucking meal. Leon was a lame ass for telling her my damn business. I was devastated and embarrassed because the whole entire neighborhood was outside watching the scene. Leon couldn't say shit but sorry. He knew he was cold busted, red-handed. Of course, he got me to stay. To this day, I don't know why I did.

I knew Leon and I hadn't met under the greatest of circumstances. I had been fucking one of his other friends when I started messing with Leon behind his friend's back. Although that was foul, I had never disrespected Leon in public or by having any cats I fucked with confront him. My past before him was something he had to deal with. If he didn't want me, a girl who had fucked half of Norfolk, then he shouldn't have made me wifey.

After the first cheating incident with Leon, it was like the flood gates opened with him and other chicks. Leon was the disrespectful type of cheater. As foul as it sounded, I wished he would have kept his shit on the low, out of sight, out of mind. No, not his trifling ass. He had bitches calling my house and coming over to curse me out. He would stay out nights with no explanation and come home smelling like stale pussy and perfume.

And my stupid ass put up with all that bullshit. I stayed through it all, but I completely checked out of our relationship. I stopped cooking for him, washing his clothes, or working to help him pay bills. I felt like, *if you want to be a fucking dog, then you take care of yourself.*

Of course, Leon used that shit against me. When we did the spouse trade, Troy told me that Leon called me lazy and that I refused to help him pay bills. Leon painted the picture that I just sat around eating all day doing nothing. Hearing that shit hurt me, but of course, I played tough like it didn't. Leon liked to tell one side of the story, but he never told on himself. He never told the reason I stopped doing shit for him was because he was a low-down dirty dog.

But the most fucked-up time of all was now. Of all the times he had cheated, this was the fucking worst I'd ever felt.

He was locked the fuck up and still being a motherfucking dog. And with this bitch Trice no less! No, this wouldn't be the last time Leon would hear from me. I was going to make sure of that.

I finally pulled myself together. After thinking back on shit and all the things Leon put me through, I roughly wiped the tears from my face and I went from hurt to full-out mad as hell. I inhaled a deep breath and started my car. I had someplace important to go before I went home. I was already calculating my plan for revenge. My mind raced a mile a minute.

I kept picturing Trice's face in my mind. Then

I would see Leon's. Those images just fueled the fire raging inside of me.

"You want to fuck with me, Leon? You wait and see what I have in store for your mother-fucking ass!" I gritted through clenched teeth as I pulled away from the prison.

"And, Trice, you bitch, you just wait. You think you skated death once, well, you won't skate a second time, bitch! I fucking promise you that shit," I hissed as I clutched the steering wheel so tight my busted knuckles burned.

It was going to be on and popping now. I was driving like a bat out of hell to my destination. My insides churned with anticipation of what was to come. I had a whole new fucking mission in mind. Trice and Leon had fucked over the wrong bitch!

The saying goes that there is nothing worse than a woman scorned. Well, I was about to show Leon and Trice that there was nothing worse than fucking over Charlene!

They want a fight, well, Charlene is declaring a motherfucking war. Believe that!

7

Troy

After I watched Trice sneak out of the house and drive away, I knew something was up for sure. She left around six o'clock on a Saturday morning, so where would an eight-months pregnant woman be going at that time of morning? Not to mention, she was all dressed up, with makeup on and all. I was incensed. I paced around my bedroom for almost thirty minutes, not knowing what move to make next. Trice and I had agreed to go see an insurance broker to get our finances in order before the baby comes. Either she forgot or she didn't care.

I called her sister, Anna, but she said she hadn't seen or heard from Trice. That made me even madder. Anna was the only family Trice had.

Their mother had abandoned them a long time ago, and her father was an alcoholic who wasted no time molesting his two daughters. Trice and Anna had run away and basically raised themselves from pillar to post.

When I met Trice, she was in school and working. I was impressed with her, especially after she told me of her rough upbringing. She had been so different from the usual no-ambition chicks I knew and occasionally dealt with. I instantly fell for her. Shit kind of went downhill right after we married, though.

Trice didn't want to have sex with me as often as she did when we were dating, and she always complained about everything I did. Nothing was ever good enough for her, and the further we got in our marriage, the worse the complaints got. I initially attributed the lack of sex to her father molesting her, and somehow I was convinced the complaints were connected to her mom abandoning her. That was bullshit. I was making excuses for her ass.

Now she had resorted to sneaking out of the house. Something was definitely going on, and I intended to find out what it was. I finally got dressed after not being able to reach Trice on her phone. I went to the insurance appointment alone. I upped our life insurance to one million dollars' worth of coverage on each of us with a rider that would cover the baby for thirty thousand dollars until she was of age to get her own coverage.

Bernie, the insurance salesman, kept making references to my wife not being there, which was embarrassing. I had tried to smile and play it off, but I was seething inside. He gave me papers for Trice to sign. She would have to agree to the insurance amounts before the policy would be effective.

When I arrived back home, her ass still wasn't home. I called her cell again, and it went directly to voice mail. It was almost six hours since I'd seen her with no call or contact. As mad as I was, I was really starting to worry. I couldn't sit still in the house, so I grabbed my car keys and headed out. I planned to scour the city to see if I saw her car or any sign of her.

The first place I went was the hair salon Trice frequented. I didn't see her car in the lot, and I didn't want to go inside and make myself look stupid, so I walked past the window to see if I could see inside, but the salon had too many hair posters plastered over the glass to really get a good glimpse inside. I figured if her car wasn't there, she wasn't there.

Next, I drove to Captain George's Seafood Restaurant, which was Trice's favorite place to eat. I drove through the crowded parking lot and didn't see her car there either. I went to banks, malls, movie theaters, and her OB-GYN's office. I couldn't find her anywhere. The entire time I searched, I would stop periodically and call her cell phone. I had left her so many messages that her mailbox was eventually too full to accept any more. It wasn't like Trice to disappear like this without so much as a call.

Finally, I relented and decided to head back home. I prayed all the way home that Trice would be there with a good explanation for her disappearance when I arrived. I had a windstorm of emotions spinning in my heart. I drove as slowly as I could through Virginia Beach, just in case I ran into her.

When I got to my house, I noticed a green Honda Accord parked across the street. It struck me as strange because all of our neighbors parked in their driveways. I pulled into my empty driveway and got out of my car. Before I could make it all the way up my front stairs, I heard heels clacking on the ground behind me. I turned around to investigate.

The occupant of the green Honda was headed in my direction. My face instantly folded into a scowl, and my hands curled into fists at my sides. My eyes squinted into little dashes.

"What the fuck do you want, Charlene?" I hissed, ready for a confrontation.

Charlene was nothing but trouble. She had caused enough grief and drama in my life, and I hated the sight of this scandalous bitch.

"Look, I ain't come here for no drama. I came

to tell you what the fuck I know about your perfect little wife and my trifling-ass husband," Charlene spat, her face looking crazy. I could tell she'd been crying, because her makeup was smeared and her eyes were red.

"I don't want to hear shit you got to say. You lied once and you'll lie again," I said dismissively, getting ready to give her my back. She was the one who'd lied about her and I having sex and ruined our chances of getting any money from the *Trading Spouses* show and everyone's lives. I wasn't trying to hear shit she had to say. "You can't be trusted."

"Oh, yeah, well, I bet you Trice ain't home. I bet you she left . . . hmmm, let's see, around six o'clock this morning. I bet you she was all dressed up and that she's still gone," Charlene replied spitefully.

Her words were hitting me like a ton of bricks. She was right on point. I stopped moving. I wanted to hear what she had to say now.

No, I had to hear what she had to say now.

"Oh, see, I thought you would want to hear what the fuck I have to say now," Charlene continued crossly. She had her head cocked to the side as she tapped her foot. That was like the hood rat's national anthem, head cocked to the side and foot tapping. Any professional and sophisticated sisters did that same shit when they finally reached their boiling point.

"Just get to the point, Charlene," I told her.

Charlene squinted her eyes into little beads. "Oh, I'm gon' get to the motherfucking point all right. It seems that your pretty little perfect wife is seeing my husband on his visits," she started.

It was like she had just slapped me across the face.

"What? Get the fuck out of here, Charlene! Your husband almost fucking killed Trice. Why would she be visiting him?" I snapped. I was ready to kick this bitch off my property for coming up with that bullshit story.

"Oh, you don't wanna believe that Ms. Perfect can't be grimy as hell? Okay, well stay there and be a dumb fuck if you want to, but according to what I just learned, this bitch goes to see Leon every Tuesday and I've been going on Saturdays. But this week, I told Leon I wasn't coming. He must've told her that I wasn't coming, so Trice took my visiting day."

"I can't believe that shit without some proof," I retorted, growing angrier by the minute.

"I wasn't stupid enough to come to you without fucking proof, Troy. Today, when I showed up to surprise Leon, they wouldn't let me in. I'm like, what the fuck is going on? And boom! I find out from the CO that Ms. Trice Davis signed in on both visits this week. Today included," Charlene explained.

I was speechless and just kept staring at her. It

was as if her words were punches to my gut and more slaps to my face. I was breathing rapidly and clenching my jaw so hard I was starting to get a headache.

"Mmm-hmm. Your wife, Trice Davis, visited my husband. The one who, as you said, almost killed the bitch," Charlene said, whirling her head around on her neck like a damn carousel. "If you don't believe me, take this as proof." Charlene shoved a folded-up piece of paper toward my chest. I grabbed the paper and unfolded it. It was a printout of Leon's prison log, and just like Charlene had said, Trice's name was there—twice. My hands were shaking. A lump the size of a tennis ball formed at the back of my throat.

"Oh, and I also found out that she puts money on his account. I hadn't had the chance to put money on this week, but I got one of my friends who works inside to pull his records—somebody made a deposit of a hundred dollars today."

Charlene kept dishing the dirt and stabbing me deeper and deeper in my heart with information. I couldn't even say shit. My ears were ringing, and I felt like I could just kill someone with my bare hands. Charlene was tapping her foot as if she expected me to hug and kiss her for giving me the information.

"You can thank me later. And if I were you, I would get rid of that trifling bitch. Shit, for all you know, she could be setting your ass up for the downfall. Leon is very slick and apparently so is your wife," Charlene said cruelly.

"There must be some explanation for this. Trice is pregnant with our daughter, and she wouldn't be going to any prison!" I snapped. I couldn't let her know that she was getting to me. As much shit I had given her, no way she needed to know how big an idiot I was.

"Pregnant? Oh, yeah, well, if you count the months, she might just be pregnant with Leon's baby and not yours," Charlene said maliciously.

It was like I suddenly became possessed by the devil. The more Charlene spoke, the angrier I got and the more I wanted to take her head off along with Trice's. Charlene was the fucking messenger and yes, I wanted to kill the messenger for the multiple daggers she just stabbed me with. Because every dirty deed Trice had done was a dagger. And just my luck, the deliverer of those daggers was Charlene, of all damn people.

"Get the fuck away from my house and don't come back! I don't want to see you around here! Get the fuck away from here!" I barked.

Charlene's eyes grew wide. I must've looked like a scary killer, because she stepped backward so fast, she almost fell flat on her ass in those heels.

"Call me if you want more information!" Charlene exclaimed. "And I would get a paternity test if I were you!"

"Whatever, bitch! Get the fuck out of here!" I screamed at her back. There was no way I could let Charlene see that the information she gave me had just killed me inside. It all made sense now. All of Trice's disappearing acts, her sneaky behavior, and her nasty behavior toward me. It was all because she was still seeing Leon, a fucking convict, behind my back. The same motherfucker who damn near killed her and the baby. And the thought that the baby may not be mine was what really had me boiling inside.

I rushed into the house and I couldn't help it. I ran upstairs to our bedroom and just started wrecking Trice's shit. I swiped all of her makeup and expensive perfumes from her dresser and vanity. I went into our closet and started throwing all of her shit out the door. I wrecked her neat stacks of shoeboxes and tore some of her expensive dresses from the hangers. I was sweating and my chest was heaving when I finally stopped.

After a few minutes, I stood amid the wreckage and put my head in my hands. I squeezed my head and tried to get my thoughts together.

"What the fuck are you doing, Troy?" I asked myself out loud. "This is something a bitch would do to her cheating man. Men get revenge in other ways. Man the fuck up! Man the fuck up for once!" I chanted to myself.

I looked around at the complete and utter mess I had made of Trice's things. It was really a sight to see. Clothes, shoes, coats, handbags, perfume, and makeup were all over the floor. It was all shit I had bought for Trice to begin with. I shook my head at how bitchy I was acting by wrecking her stuff. I had heard from other brothers about how we men just lose ourselves when a woman truly hurt us. They say we become just as bitchy as women. Shit, I was another statistic.

I exhaled deeply and quickly pulled myself together. I rushed to pick everything up before Trice got back home. I put her perfumes and cosmetics back as best I could. Some of the bottles were broken into pieces, but I quickly thought of a lie to tell her to explain. I finished cleaning up her shit in the nick of time. I heard her car pull into the driveway just as I finished.

I went into the bathroom and counted to ten as I looked at myself in the mirror. I was silently praying that when I saw her face, I would be able to control myself and ask her where she'd been. I was afraid if she lied to my face, I wouldn't be able to control what would happen next.

I really felt like I could kill that bitch and have no remorse.

8

Leon

The CO in the visitors' room had warned me not to have physical contact with Trice when they saw me touching her stomach. That damn baby had gone crazy under my touch, and it just made me feel like shit knowing that I wouldn't be there for the birth of my first daughter. I was in a fucked-up position and felt powerless. Then, on top of everything else, to know that my former best friend would be playing daddy to my daughter, my insides felt like pure shit. My manhood was being tested on so many levels.

I left the visit with Trice feeling all conflicted and shit. She had flat-out told me she wasn't trying to stop living with Troy. Wasn't that a bitch? I mean, I understood her point, but it didn't make it easy to accept. It drove me fucking nuts. I could just picture them playing fucking house with my seed. Troy thinking it was his baby and he being the one to bond with my daughter. Trice would be there like the happy wife and mother, smiling and acting as if nothing were an issue. She was a great actress—I had to give her that.

I was starting to feel like Trice was grimier than Charlene. I mean, I wasn't complaining, but she was actually still carrying on a relationship with me while she lived with Troy. I think I would kill a bitch for something like that.

Troy didn't have the heart, though. He had always been the soft one when we were growing up. If he found out about me and Trice, that nigga would probably lie in a corner and cry and then beg Trice to stay with him. That was his nature—a punk-ass nigga. I guess that was why Trice was able to get away with our little thing we had going on. I had to be careful with her ass, because I've seen firsthand what she was capable of. The difference between Trice and Charlene was Trice was smart and calculating with her shit and Charlene was too dumb to hide shit.

I got back to my cell and found Kenny lying on his bunk. He gritted on me, but I slid into my bunk and ignored that nigga.

I was in the cell for about fifteen minutes when I heard the prison horn going off. I jumped up because I knew that meant they were coming to shake down someone's cell. The COs would do random cell searches if they suspected contraband had been let into the prison. I sighed loudly and began to walk to the doorway of my cell to see who was going to be the lucky motherfucker getting their shit destroyed by the COs.

"Turn around and place your hands up! Now!" I heard screams coming from several different directions, and I was suddenly rushed by about ten COs dressed in their riot gear.

"What the fuck, man?" I screamed. I was roughly dragged out of my cell and placed in handcuffs. The remaining COs from the ESU trampled into my cell and began throwing shit around like they always do during a cell search. I was laid on my stomach on the floor of the cellblock, three cells down from mine. I saw all my shit flying out of the cell, including my mattress, toiletries, pictures, books, and commissary food. They were searching through everything. They ripped open food packages, searched the mattress and toilet. They even ripped open the little bullshit-ass pillow they gave us.

"Found it!" I heard one of the COs yell. I started squirming on the floor. The next thing I knew, I was being roughly hoisted up off the floor and dragged.

"Bunch, you are under re-arrest for the possession of contraband," one of them said to me.

I began bucking my body like crazy. "What? I don't have shit in that cell! Y'all must've planted some shit! What the fuck is going on?" I screamed as I was being dragged away. Just as I passed my cell, I locked eyes with Kenny. That motherfucker had a coy smile on his face.

"You snitch! You fucking set me up! You bitch-ass nigga! Snitches don't survive behind these walls!" I yelled at Kenny. He just looked at me and didn't reply. He must have planted something in my cell while I was on my visit. Then the motherfucker went to the CO and dropped a dime. They probably gave his ass a few days off of his sentence for his cooperation. I couldn't fucking believe he had stooped that low.

I was brought down to the punitive segregation unit or better known as the fucking hole. They stripped off my jumpsuit and left me in just boxers and a T-shirt. I was shoved into the single cell and the metal door was closed behind me. There was nothing in the cell but a slab of concrete with a very thin plastic thing that was supposed to serve as a mattress. There was no blanket, pillow, or television, and worst of all, the door was solid, so there was no seeing out. The light was dim as shit, as there was no window for sunlight. I already felt like I was going fucking crazy in there. I put my head in my hands for a few minutes and then I looked around again.

"Agggghh!" I screamed angrily. Then I punched the cinder-block wall. "Agggh!" I screamed again when I felt the bones in my hand shatter. I was in pain, but more so angry to the point that I could kill someone. This shit meant war. I was definitely going to get Kenny's ass back for this one. That nigga was as good as dead in my eyes.

9

Trice

The visit with Leon was stressful to say the least.
He started talking crazy, asking me to leave Troy,
because he didn't want Troy raising our baby or
me playing house with Troy. I had to tell Leon
how I felt about that shit. I made it quite clear
that he was not calling the shots from behind
prison walls. Not to mention, I had to point out
to him that he was in prison for shooting me!

However, Leon and I didn't end our visit
angry with each other. He had lovingly caressed
my belly and felt the baby moving inside of me.
Of course, he was reprimanded for touching
me. Something about Leon not being able to
rub my stomach and feel his own baby move

made me know at that moment that staying with Troy was definitely the right thing to do.

Before I left the visitors' area, everyone was held up for what the COs explained was a lockdown situation at the prison. That shit held me up for at least forty-five minutes. I was beginning to get very nervous. My mind was racing with thoughts about Troy looking for me. I knew he had figured out that I left the house fairly early. How would I explain being gone until the evening? I was a bag of nerves when we were finally turned loose. Those damn COs had searched us over and over again. That whole ordeal counted as another strike against having a man in prison. I didn't take kindly to being treated as if I were the prisoner myself.

When I reached my car, I turned my cell phone on and at least fifteen voice mails, thirty text messages, and numerous missed calls from Troy flooded my phone. I had to think up something by the time I reached the house. My hands shook like crazy as I fumbled with my phone. I listened to message after message. I knew Troy very well. I knew he'd be angry, which for Troy meant he would want to have a long talk about his feelings. I could definitely handle that.

In between his messages was one from my sister, Anna. I decided to call her back and just deal with Troy when I got home. Anna picked up on the second ring.

"Trice! Where the hell are you?" Anna yelled into the phone. Shit, she scared me.

"Why are you all frantic? I went to the hair salon and then I went window-shopping for baby stuff. Why?" I replied, my eyebrows furrowed in confusion.

"Girl, Troy called here looking for you. He said you left at six this morning and were nowhere to be found. Trice, what is going on over there?" Anna said all in one big breath.

"Oh, please. I didn't think he would put out a search party for me. I'm on my way home now. I'll deal with him when I get there. I'm fine. He'll be fine too. You know I know how to handle that man," I told her. I chuckled afterward to lighten the mood. It was probably more a nervous laugh than a true laugh.

"You better stop whatever it is that you're doing. Troy is far from stupid," Anna said, her tone ominous. I rolled my eyes and shook my head. My sister was working my nerves now.

"Not you too," I retorted. "Look, I gotta go. I can't stand all of this probing into my business. Later." I clicked the phone off. I didn't even give her a chance to give me one of her infamous lectures. I just wasn't up for it.

I had listened to all of Troy's messages. Anna might be right. Troy's messages started off sounding nice, but by the time he left the last message, his tone reminded me of a maniac. I shrugged my shoulders and waved it off. I knew Troy was all bark and no bite. He was weak as hell, and I knew how to work my magic on his ass. I had my story prepared and ready to tell to his simple ass. He would have to get up very early in the morning to be a step ahead of me. I was much smarter than Troy.

When I arrived home, his car was there. Even though I wasn't worried about what he thought, my heart still started racing when I saw the car. I guess it was a mixture of anxiety and guilt. I had been gone all day. I felt a little guilty for having Troy worry about me like that. If he called Anna, that meant he was on the verge of going nuts.

I shrugged again and exhaled the deep breath I had just taken in. I wanted to be calm when I spoke to him. I climbed out of my car and walked up to the house slowly. My feet were kind of swollen from being out all day. Plus, the baby had been pushing on my bladder since I had left the prison. Shit, eight months pregnant wasn't a joke.

I looked at the windows first, and an eerie feeling hit me in the pit of my stomach. Although Troy's car was in the driveway, there were absolutely no lights illuminating the windows. I swallowed hard and put my key into the lock. I slowly pushed the door in once the lock gave. The entire house was pitch-black. All the curtains and shades were drawn and none of the lights were on. *Shit, he must be upstairs.* I kicked off my shoes, threw my handbag on the table next to the door, and inched my way inside. I was headed toward the light switch on the wall so I could see and make my way to the kitchen. I didn't know if it was still my nerves or what, but for some reason I was tiptoeing as lightly as I could. I actually felt like I was doing something wrong in my own house.

I reached out my hand to feel for the light switch, and then the shock of my life almost made my water break.

"Did you have a good day out?" Troy's voice boomed from behind me. I jumped so hard a little bit of pee escaped my bladder and went down the inside of my pants and thighs. I whirled around on the balls of my feet and almost lost my balance. I stumbled to catch myself before I hit the floor.

"Oh my God! Troy! You scared me so bad!" I gasped. I was breathing so hard I instantly felt light-headed. My heart raced so rapidly I thought it would come up out of my throat. I gripped my belly because a sharp pain hit me there like a thunderbolt. Maybe it was my shocked state, but I was sure Troy made no move to catch me when I was stumbling. I could have fallen and lost the baby and he'd have just sat there. I hoped it was just my imagination.

"I didn't mean to scare you. Just wanted to ask about your day," Troy droned. His voice was strange. He sounded eerily calm and robotic. Kind of maniacal, if you asked me.

"Well, you did scare me," I huffed. "And I think I just had a contraction because of it." Troy stayed sitting in the same spot in the dark. I could only see his silhouette.

"Did you hear what I just said, Troy? I'm having pains!" I screamed at him.

"I'm sorry, Trice. I didn't mean to cause you any pain." His voice still droned in that same crazy-sounding voice.

I stomped over to the light switch behind one of the end tables and clicked it on. I looked over at Troy, and he was just staring straight ahead. My face was bunched into the ugliest scowl. I was trying to flip the script on him. I thought I could immediately make an issue out of him scaring me and it would take the focus off my six-hour absence.

"What is going on with you?" I asked angrily. I knew how to gear up for my act. It had worked so many times on Troy I had lost count.

"I went to the insurance appointment today without you. I need you to sign these papers so the baby will have insurance," Troy told me. He was acting as if I never said anything to him. He never answered my questions.

I looked down on the coffee table and saw the paperwork scattered all over it. "I'll sign them after I read them," I replied. "You can't go around scaring me. I don't know why you insist on sneaking up on me like you have some kind of problem." I had put on my angriest face, and I knew my chastising would eventually get to him. This was the berating phase of my plan. Troy usually would apologize and start begging me for forgiveness whenever I did this to him.

However, I sensed that this time was different. "I don't appreciate the way you act, Troy. Like a detective." I was rambling like a mother correcting a child. Although he was still stoic sitting in the chair, he had to be feeling low from my onslaught. I even had my pointer finger trained on him, wagging it in his face.

Then it happened. He snapped. It was as if Anna's premonition was coming true. Troy was on his feet so swiftly I didn't even have time to flinch. He rushed into me, sending me stumbling onto the couch. He put his hands around my throat and began to squeeze tightly.

"No, Trice! You will sign the motherfucking papers now!" his voice exploded as he choked the shit out of me. "I'm not playing any more fucking games with you . . . Sign them now!"

I was flabbergasted and taken aback. Troy was squeezing so hard I thought my windpipe would crumble to pieces under his clutch. Tears were streaming out of my eyes. I was scared to death. I had never seen him act this way. In all of the years we had been married, he had never put his hands on me in a violent or rough way.

I started clawing at his hands around my throat, but I was no match for his strength. "Your little angry act is not going to fucking work this time, you lying bitch! You better sign these papers right now or you may not live to see another sneaking, trifling, fucking day," Troy growled. Little dots of his spit were flying in my face. His eyes looked like someone had lit a fire inside of them.

"Please, Troy," I rasped as I looked into his eyes. He looked like pure evil at that moment. "I'll sign them," I managed to get out, my voice muffled by his grip. Finally, he released me. I started coughing like crazy and panting.

Troy grabbed the papers off the table and flung them at me. "Sign them now!" his voice roared as the papers scattered all over the floor and me.

I was crying hysterically now. I gathered the papers while my hands shook fiercely. I could barely hold the pen. Troy stood over me brooding like a madman. I looked up at him pitifully.

"Sign!" he boomed again, flexing his body toward me. I flinched and with shaking hands, I scribbled my signature on all the pages that had little yellow *sign here* tabs. I had no idea what I was even signing. Troy snatched the papers from me when I was done, causing me to throw my arms up in defense. I was still having pains in my belly like crazy. I wasn't sure if he was going to hit me again or what. He looked over the insurance papers and then he scowled at me.

"Whatever you did today, I hope it was all worth it, Trice," he said in an almost-inaudible whisper. I was too afraid to hold eye contact with him. I put my head down and let the tears run. *What have I done? What have I gotten myself into?* My mind raced with all sorts of thoughts.

Troy shook his head and grimaced like he was disgusted with me. I thought he was one second from spitting on me as if I were the lowest piece of scum on earth.

Then he stomped away from me without another word. I couldn't help but wonder why Troy never asked me where I had been all day. It was as if he already knew I was going to lie. I was too scared to even move a muscle, much less tell him the lie I had prepared in my head.

10

Charlene

Two days had passed since I found out about Leon and Trice. I found it real strange that Leon hadn't called me either. I couldn't help but think he somehow knew that I had found out. I had placed a couple of calls to my people at the prison to probe around, but I hadn't gotten any calls back yet. I knew I would eventually get to the bottom of it, but I still couldn't help but wonder if that wimpy-ass Troy had gone crying to Trice and told her about my little visit and her ass getting busted visiting my fucking husband.

It had been hard for me to get up and go to the club with the way I had been feeling. But as usual, Charlene the trouper had to pull it together or else my son and I wouldn't eat or have a place to live. It was just that fucking simple. Once again, I had to pick up the slack where Leon's trifling ass had left it.

I had been dragging myself around my small apartment, throwing costumes in my bag, shaving, and getting myself ready for another long night at the club when my cell phone started buzzing on my nightstand. I slid into my tight jeans and grabbed the phone.

"Yeah," I answered rudely. I just wasn't in the mood to speak to anyone at all. I knew it wouldn't be Leon calling, because he always called me on my house phone.

"Charlene?" the voice on the other end asked. My eyebrows shot up at the fact that it was a man on the line. I wasn't fucking with nobody and nobody had my real number like that. The cell phone I used was Leon's old cell he used prior to him pulling time.

"Yeah . . . who is this?" I asked, scrunching up my face. I wasn't up for strange fucking phone calls or any bullshit tonight.

"I need to speak with you in person," the voice said.

I pulled the phone from my ear and looked at the screen. The number had been blocked, which I hadn't checked before I picked up the phone. I cocked my head to the side as if to say, *No the fuck he didn't.* I mean, how could someone say they need to see me and not even tell me who in the hell it was.

"Who in the fuck is this, first of all?" I snapped. I thought for a minute the voice sounded familiar.

"Come on, Charlene, you lived with me once, remember? It's Troy," he said it like he was all annoyed and shit.

"Well, just because I lived with you for a week doesn't mean I'm going to remember how you sound over the phone. You are the last person I expected to hear from after how you acted the other day," I began chastising his ass. "I was only trying to help you keep from getting played like a fool. I don't have time for games. If you called to curse me out again, no thank you. Shit, a bitch was only trying to help your silly ass out."

"I know. That's why I am calling. I wanted to apologize for my behavior," Troy stated, sounding sincere as hell. "I was just caught way off guard, and I didn't expect you to have proof of what you were telling me about Trice and Leon. You of all people should understand how it could all be a misunderstanding, right? I mean, there have been so many lies exchanged since the show, I just don't know what to believe."

I could tell from his voice he was a broken man after what I had revealed to him. I guess he had finally seen Trice for what she was—a lying, scheming, trifling-ass bitch. And it was true—men were more broken than women when they found out some other man had been pounding their pussy.

I kind of felt good about Troy's discovery of

that scandalous bitch. It had hurt me a lot to know that both Leon and Troy had wanted Trice in the end. To tell you the truth, it caused me to really want revenge on all of them: Trice, Leon, and Troy.

"Hmm, that's all you calling for? To apologize?" I asked skeptically. I was a very good reader of people, and I could tell there was some ulterior motive lurking behind Troy's phone call. I was impatiently tapping my foot in anticipation of him coming clean about his real intentions for the call. "I'm waiting," I said.

This nigga started stammering. "Um . . . um . . ."

I knew it, just like I thought, something behind the call.

"I . . . I wanted to see if we could meet up. I wanted to speak to you some more about this little dilemma we're both in," Troy stuttered.

Hell, I was finally happy he got his words out. I had my mouth twisted. I knew game when I heard it. Troy didn't want to meet with me to exchange heartbreak stories, and I knew that for sure. There had to be more to it.

"No. I'm sorry, but I'm not in anyone's dilemma. Leon's ass is the one locked up and can't do shit for me," I told him. "I will get my revenge on his ass one way or another. You, on the other hand, got yourself a fucking problem. Shit, now that I know there is a baby involved, you got more problems than me, for sure. I would be looking for revenge if I was you." As sick and fucked up as it was, I was enjoying verbally pouring salt on his wounds.

Troy cleared his throat. "Yeah, revenge is exactly what I wanted to speak to you about," he replied. That shocked me. Troy didn't seem like the vengeful type. I was all ears now.

"Okay, I'm listening," I said. I was still wondering why he wanted to tell me, of all people, about wanting to get revenge on Trice. Maybe he figured I hated that bitch just as much as he did.

"Nah, we can't speak over the telephone. It has to be in person. I can meet you wherever you say. It's important that it be someplace we can speak privately without a lot of ears around," Troy told me.

I raised my eyebrows at that too. He had my interest piqued, although I was kind of wondering, why in the hell it needed to be ultra-private to talk about what spiteful shit we could do to get back at our spouses. Damn his ass was paranoid.

"I hear you. I work tonight at the Glass Slipper. There's a private champagne room in the back where we can speak, but you'll have to pay because you'll be taking money out of my pocket if I spend time in private with you."

Internally, I laughed at my own scheming. This was business for Troy, but it was also a ploy for me. I was thinking I could kill two birds with one stone—hear what Troy had to say and try to get his ass to finally lay it on me so I could be fully even with Leon's cheating ass.

Troy blew out a long breath like my idea was dumb. That instantly pissed me off. He wasn't going to be asking a favor and calling the shots at the same time. Just like a damn man to want his cake and eat it too. They just had to be the damn shot-callers. Well, not this time dammit. I was no longer having anyone treat me that fucking way. Leon had done enough damage from me letting him call the shots all the time. The new and improved Charlene was not putting her feelings on the back burner for anyone else ever again.

"Look, if you don't want to come to the club, then I don't know what to tell you. I don't have time for games. You called me with this bullshit. Remember that. I gotta go," I plainly stated. I was about to bang that damn phone on his ass.

"No. No. Wait. I'm going to come. Just tell me what time to be there. I'll have on dark glasses and a Norfolk State University skull cap pulled down low," Troy replied, his words coming out fast and nervous. I smiled a little bit at the control I had over the situation. I couldn't front—it made me feel powerful. Damn right, he better come correct.

"All right. I'll see you tonight at eleven-thirty. I hope whatever you got to talk to me about is worth my time, because in my line of work, time is money and money is time," I kindly informed Troy. I wasn't joking either. He better not go there for some straight-up bullshit, because I knew how scary and dumb Troy could be. I had learned that firsthand during the spouse trade when I tried fifty different ways to throw my pussy at him and he bolted from it like he was a damn runaway slave.

I started thinking devilishly about our meeting. I wondered if this last time would be a charm with Troy. Maybe getting him to give in this time wouldn't be so hard, since I would have his ass at my mercy.

I hung up the phone and flopped back on my bed. I kicked my legs in the air. "Yes! Yes! Yes! You fucking wait, Leon. You just wait until you get your next package from me! I got big plans for you, nigga!" I said excitedly.

Revenge was a dish best fucking served cold and that was a fact for sure!

"You better get your ass to that club, Charlene. You got a big night ahead of you," I said to myself jokingly as I grabbed my shit, kissed my son, paid my babysitter, and headed out the door.

11

Troy

My call with Charlene didn't start off easy, which I expected, but it ended well. I was actually kind of excited that she agreed to meet with me, albeit at the strip club. I didn't even tell Trice I was leaving the house or where I was going. That wasn't like me at all. So I knew she felt it. I was also sure she knew how much I didn't like or respect her ass anymore. In some ways, she was dead to me emotionally. One day that may change, but for now I didn't give a fuck.

And I certainly didn't give a fuck about how she felt lately in light of the information I had. Trice had no idea what I knew. She had been tiptoeing around me since the day she got busted.

She had also been really sweet toward me for the past couple of days. She had even tried to seduce me. Imagine that! My wife, who hasn't wanted to have sex with me in eight months, suddenly wanted to fuck me. I had pushed her used ass away and told her I wasn't in the mood. She had looked like a puppy that had just got kicked in the side. I didn't care how sad she looked. As far as I was concerned, all of her little efforts at reconciliation with me were too little, too fucking late. Each time I laid eyes on her, I felt like I could just take her fucking head off her shoulders. All of her phony niceness just made me angrier. Fucking bitch!

I usually rubbed her stomach, back, and feet, but now I couldn't stand the thought of touching or comforting her when she might be carrying another man's baby. A few times I even pictured myself beating her ass to death with my bare hands. I was deeply hurt and that hurt had definitely turned into hatred.

I had lost control and I know that shit should have scared me. That night she returned from the prison, I was full of emotions. I wanted to play it cool. But when her stupid ass tried to turn that shit on me, I snapped. I don't think she realized how close she came to being six feet under and me catching a case for killing her cheating ass.

And I knew how lucky I was she didn't call the cops. My handprints were all over her neck, and the fact that she was pregnant would have definitely put me behind bars the whole weekend, if not longer.

I arrived at the Glass Slipper at eleven-thirty just like Charlene had instructed. I kept my dark sunglasses on and pulled my hat low until it practically covered my eyebrows. I had rarely frequented strip clubs, so when I walked inside, I could feel my eyes widen involuntarily behind my shades. The club was dark and even darker with my shades on. There was a thick, dull gray cloud of smoke hanging in the air and the entire place reeked of smoke, cheap perfume, and sweat. The smoke instantly made my mouth pasty and dry. I guess the fact that I was nervous also didn't help.

My heart was beating fast with anticipation as I looked around to see if I could spot Charlene. There were so many naked women there and it was dark, especially with the dark shades on. I couldn't make out any of the women with all the different types of wigs on and shit. I couldn't be sure which one was Charlene, especially from behind, since it seemed like they all had nice-size juicy booties. I saw some beautiful women, nice asses, and pretty tits. Then there were some that made me question why a strip club would hire them. I swore I saw one chick with a bullet hole in her damn leg and so much cellulite her entire ass jiggled like a bowl of Jell-O when she walked.

I finally sat down in a corner by a table that

had a sign that read *VIP* on it, just like Charlene had told me to do. I wasn't even fully in the seat when a slim Latina with oversized breasts and a small waist approached me. She was completely nude. I could feel my dick start to pulse a little bit in my pants as I looked her up and down. She was like a ghetto J.Lo. I would have given it to her ass, for sure.

"You want a private dance?" the girl asked seductively. Then she pinched her own nipples and licked one of them herself. Damn! That was some shit I had never seen before. I laughed nervously. It was how I always reacted when I was excited and nervous at the same time.

"Um . . . no . . . I'm waiting for somebody," I stammered. The girl started pinching her nipples even harder to entice me. She moaned seductively too. Now my dick went from pulsing to rock hard within a matter of seconds. I instantly wanted to fuck. I had to shake it off and remember why I was there.

Thank God, Charlene saved me just in time.

"He's waiting for me! Get the fuck out of my section, Marisol! I done told you before that this is all me over here—don't make me fuck you up!" Charlene screamed from behind us. I was startled and so was the girl. The girl looked at me as if to say *you bastard*; then she turned with wide eyes and looked at Charlene. She didn't want any part of Charlene, so she scurried away like a dog with its tail between its legs.

I was embarrassed because I knew Charlene could tell I had a hard dick. I turned to face her. I lowered my sunglasses and peeked at her over the top of them. I took in her getup. She had on a long, jet-black wig that had a few loose curls in it. Her face was plastered with makeup—silver glitter on her eyelids, ruby-red lipstick on her full lips, and enough foundation to make Charlene look a few shades lighter than I'd remembered. She was topless and only wore a skimpy red lace G-string. She had on a pair of high, clear plastic heels—definitely come-fuck-me heels. Charlene's deep-chocolate-colored thighs gleamed with whatever oil she'd rubbed on her body. Her stomach was flat and her ass was just as round as I had remembered it.

When she'd stayed in my house for that week, she had wasted no time making sure I got to see her body. Those were the times she had tried her best to seduce me and I fought the feelings to give in, all because of my love and respect for Trice. I felt real stupid now. When it came to wives and relationships, we as men didn't believe in loyalty. My dumb ass wanted to be different— different for Trice. I wanted to kick my own ass.

But now my eyes were open. Like it was the first time, I was seeing just how sexy Charlene really was. Looking at her didn't do anything to help tame my rock-hard dick. I tried to put my hand over it, but she could tell.

"Troy, you are staring . . . more like drooling

at me," she said, breaking my trance on that ass. Then she looked down at my groin area. I saw a sly smile form on her face. Simultaneously, I could also feel the heat of embarrassment settling on my face. It was a damn good thing the club was almost pitch-black or else I'd look mighty stupid blushing over a woman at my damn age.

"I'm sorry, Charlene. It's just that I never . . . well, you know, never seen you like this before," I replied.

Charlene laughed and then she whirled around so I could get a real good look at her. Damn, I had to admit she was some kind of sexy.

"I hope you like what you see," she cooed in a sweet husky voice. "You know, in that one week we stayed together, you could've seen me like this a million times, but you wanted to remain loyal to a bitch that is nothing but a trick." Her words stung me like a hard slap to the face. But she was right. Trice couldn't possibly love me as much as I loved her.

As Charlene and I stood there, a huge, square-shouldered nigga walked by and gave us a disapproving eye. Charlene noticed him just like I did and she quickly reacted.

"Come on, time is money in this club. We already been standing here talking too long," she said, nodding toward the dude. I guess he was the enforcer that made sure the girls didn't waste time.

"We can finish in one of the champagne rooms in the back." She grabbed me by the arm. "Let me give you a private dance, Daddy," Charlene sang, all the while looking at the big dude who had been eye-screwing us.

"I can't wait to get a piece of that ass," I said in response, playing along with Charlene's little charade. I looked at his stony face as I said it too. Charlene had to chuckle as we were walking down a long dark hallway toward the rooms where the private parties took place.

"You sound so corny, Troy," Charlene joked.

"Shhh, don't say my real name in here. You never know who is listening," I warned her.

"Oh, I forgot that you are on a top-secret mission inside of a fucking strip club," she joked. "Nigga, please. These cats back here are interested in copping a feel or better yet, trying to get some cheap pussy. They ain't hardly worried about if you came in here to discuss your cheating-ass, ho-bag wife."

I could tell I had kind of offended Charlene. She was very sensitive in that way. I thought she was joking at first. But this was her world now. Plus, I knew Leon always degraded her, treating her like shit. However, she was a woman like any other woman and liked to feel important and be put on a pedestal.

And I needed her. I was going to do whatever it took. I couldn't have her mad at me. I needed her on my side.

"Sorry, Charlene. I didn't mean anything by that," I told her.

"Whatever," she hissed. "Just get your ass inside and let's get it on."

Once we were inside the room, Charlene directed me to a small, black leather couch. There were mirrors everywhere, even on the ceiling, which kind of freaked me out. I could see myself and Charlene from every angle. It kind of made me more nervous. Candlelight was the only thing illuminating the room. It smelled as if someone had just sprayed Lysol. The smell was so strong it made me cough a little.

"Yeah, they always overdo it with the disinfectant spray, but you rather be safe than sorry. Somebody probably had their naked ass on that couch and without the disinfectant you never know."

It made sense after she explained it. I looked at a small table to the left of the couch and it contained a bottle of lubricating oil, a basket of condoms, handcuffs, and a black whip. Freaky shit. I guess the club owners expected the girls to have sex in the private rooms. Shit, I thought the rule was always "no sex in the champagne room."

"Sit down," Charlene instructed me, breaking my train of thought. I sat down gingerly on the very edge of the couch. My body was rigid, and I didn't know what to do with my hands. I was new to this. I had never been in the champagne room of any club. I had never been to something like this.

"Relax and sit back, Troy," Charlene said in a soft voice as she pushed on my shoulders, forcing me back. I fought against her pushing and tried to remain sitting up. I had a swirl of thoughts and emotions that were fighting against the pure lust that was rising inside of me just being in this environment.

"I . . . I . . . I just wanted to talk to you about something," I wolfed as Charlene kept pushing on me. The smell of her perfume was intoxicating. My dick was on swell and I could hardly catch my breath. I couldn't even remember the last time I'd had some pussy. My only release for the longest time had been jerking off. Charlene was to me at that moment what a steak would be to a starving person. I didn't know what to do with my hands. I just wanted to grab her and ram my dick hard and fast into her pussy. I tried to play it cool. "We just need to try to talk right now," I panted, trying my best to fight it.

"I know but the cameras in here need to show that we are engaged in some kind of action," Charlene whispered as she straddled me. She smiled when she felt my rock-hard manhood pressing against her pussy. I knew that would make her happy.

"I guess you're happy to see me," she cooed as she grinded her hips. Then she leaned down and whispered in my ear, "Put your hands on my ass cheeks and squeeze them so my bosses think I'm working," Charlene said, her breath hot on my ear, sending heated sparks down my back. I did as I was told. I gripped her ass cheeks with the palms of my hands and it felt good as hell. My eyes rolled up into my head without me even thinking about it.

"Aghhh," I let out a soft sigh and it was no act. I was really feeling excited.

"Now . . . tell me what you wanted to talk about," Charlene whispered seductively again as she continued to grind her pussy on my dick. I wanted to push her off so I could take it out and ram it inside of her. My hands were shaking and my heart raced as I tried to keep myself under control. I swallowed hard and attempted to get my thoughts together enough to tell her why I was there. I exhaled and squeezed Charlene's ass once more before I got to the point. Charlene was practically dry-fucking me now. She seemed to be on her own little mission just like I was.

"I want you to help me set Trice and Leon up," I told her between heavy breaths. My words didn't even faze her. She kept right on taking me there with her sexy ass.

"Oh, yeah . . . now why would I do that?" Charlene asked, and then she took her tongue and licked my ear and my neck. I could've just fainted right then. My dick was desperate for a release.

"Oh, God!" I panted. My voice was trembling, as was my entire body. "There could be a big payday in it for you. I just took out a lot of insurance on Trice," I managed to say. My eyes were closed, but I could feel Charlene stop moving.

She rose up from licking my ear and looked down in my face seriously. She stopped grinding her hips and paused for a minute. I looked at her as if to say, *Why the hell did you stop?*

"What you talking about, Troy? Insurance? You asking for help with killing Trice?" she asked in a harsh whisper. Her face was contorted, and her voice was no longer soft and sexy.

"Yeah," I replied, dead-ass serious. I had to be honest with her. Charlene's face finally lightened up. She sat back, still straddling me but not grinding on me anymore.

"Damn, nigga. I didn't think you had it in you. I'm kind of impressed and turned on at the same time." Charlene smiled cunningly. I was grateful she didn't jump up and tell me to get the fuck out. I knew I was taking a chance with Charlene, and it could've gone either way. I was hoping she was just as pissed off or more pissed off than I was. "So what made you want to finally man up?" she asked.

"I am convinced that Trice has been lying about the baby. We had sex once before she left to go stay at your house for the show, but I don't even remember coming inside of her, since she always had a fit about that," I explained honestly.

Charlene seemed to think about that for a minute. "So you think its Leon's baby for sure, then?" Her face started to turn very serious. Her eyes tightened into little dashes and she folded her arms defensively. I could tell she was starting to get angry.

"I think it's his baby, without a doubt. I think Trice has to pay the price for being a lying bitch," I gritted. "Leon, too, for that matter."

"I'm definitely down for this. How much money are we talking about?" Charlene asked. I was growing excited to hear her say she would help me. It felt good to know that my plan was about to come together.

"The policy is one million . . . if you help me, I'll give you half," I lied. How would she know I wasn't planning on giving her shit? Her eyes lit up like a kid on Christmas day.

"Shut the fuck up!" she exclaimed loudly. I reached up and covered her mouth. She quickly snapped her hand over her own mouth, realizing we were probably being watched.

"No. I'm serious," I whispered, my tone even and businesslike. "It's a good payday for you if you can set it all up. If you know people in the hood who can get it done, then I would need you to reach out to them because I don't have any connections that would work. It's too risky to solicit someone out there because a lot of times these people are undercover cops," I explained to her.

Charlene was nodding as she contemplated what I was telling her. I could see in her eyes that her mind was racing with the possibilities of what she could do with that kind of money. For now, I was proud of myself. I knew just how to appeal to a hood rat and it had worked. It was a stroke of pure genius on my part, as long as shit didn't go awry.

"I know just the right man for the job too," Charlene finally told me. I felt a pang of excitement flit through my stomach. I wanted to kiss Charlene's ass at that moment. That was exactly what I was hoping for. I certainly didn't know anyone to solicit as a damn hit man to kill my wife, but I had prayed all the way to the Glass Slipper that Charlene had some of her hood contacts that might want to make a few bucks to do it.

"Really? Who?" I asked. I was trying hard not to show too much excitement.

"I can't tell you his identity just yet or he won't do it. I have to set everything up and then he'll decide if he wants to meet with you," Charlene told me. Damn, she was on point. What she told me about the guy's identity being protected made me even more excited. That meant he was a real professional hit man with rules and shit.

"He is a regular of mine, and one night he just started telling me about what he did for a living. I'm sure I can get him to do it if the price is right," Charlene said. "But you will have to pay him before you even get the insurance money. Do you have that kind of money?" she asked skeptically.

"I can get my hands on some money from my

retirement account. Don't you worry about the money . . . I just need you to get me the man for the job," I replied.

Charlene shook her head. "A'ight, I can definitely do that shit."

"When can you set it up? I need to wait at least six weeks for the policy to be in real effect, but after that, she is open game for hunting," I said cruelly. I was really feeling like an evil bastard.

"Bet. Six weeks and you'll have your hit man," Charlene assured me. "You just became even sexier to me. I didn't know you had a bad boy bone in your body," she whispered as she began grinding on me again.

This time I grabbed her ass cheeks and forced her into me. She was sexier to me as well. I wanted to fuck the shit out of her as a thank-you for helping me. I started grinding my groin into hers. I released one of her cheeks and forced her face into mine. I wedged my tongue between her lips and kissed her deeply. Charlene had no problem returning the favor. We both let our tongues go wildly with one another. We were both damn near out of breath.

She leaned up and took my dick out of my pants through the zipper. I was grunting and panting now. I didn't know what the fuck to expect, but I knew whatever it was it would be damn good. Charlene lowered her body down as I watched her move like a snake. I used my hands and pushed the top of her head toward my dick. I knew what I was in for now. She finally got to her destination. Charlene ran her hands up and down my dick first. Then she let a wad of spit drop from her mouth onto my shaft. "Ahhh," I moaned. She then began running her hand up and down my dick rapidly, jerking me hard. I was moving my hips now. Then she did the ultimate. She stopped jerking me off and took all of my dick into her mouth.

"Oh shit!" I hissed. A familiar feeling filled my chest. I felt tingly all over my body. Now I recalled that she'd given me head during the spouse trade and it had been the best I'd ever experienced in my entire life. Charlene was making slurping noises as she practically sucked the skin off my dick. I felt so hot inside I thought I would burst.

"Oh, shit! Wait," I panted, my head going around in circles and my eyes rolled up in my head. I grabbed her head on either side and began face-fucking her. Charlene started moaning, but I wouldn't let her go. It was like I couldn't control myself. I started banging into her mouth like it was a big, wet, sloppy pussy. I was like a maniac. I hadn't had anything remotely as good as this in so fucking long. I was going crazy in her mouth. Charlene was being a trouper too. Trice would've never let me face-fuck her roughly like that. She would've never even given me head in the first damn place.

I could feel cum building up inside of me. It was

like nothing I had ever experienced. This time was ten times better than before. I guess because during the spouse trade I had fought against the feelings out of love for Trice. Not this time. I let Charlene take me to fucking ecstasy, and I didn't regret one fucking minute of it. It was coming now for sure. I banged deeper into Charlene's mouth. She wasn't even gagging, which told me she either knew how to control her gag reflex or my dick was too damn small to reach the back of her throat.

"I'm about to—" I grunted. I couldn't control it any longer. The buildup was powerful. My body was tensed. I had flexed up. It was time! "Arrggh!" I growled as a huge, hot wad of cum escaped my dick right into Charlene's mouth. "Damn! Damn! Damn!" I screeched as she sucked my dick clean. I couldn't believe it. It felt like my body was a volcano and the eruption was everlasting. And Charlene's suck was the best vacuum in the world, because every damn drop that came out, she swallowed. And every man in the world loved a woman who swallowed.

After I came, I was so damn weak. I released my grip on Charlene's head and my entire body felt relaxed. I was definitely a limp dick. Regardless of the surroundings, I just wanted to sleep. This beat jacking off any damn day of the week. Hell, I knew. For the past eight months, I had become the jacking-off champion of America. Thanks to my lovely, no-good-ass wife.

Charlene moved up so I could see her. She opened her mouth so I could see my cum on her tongue. "Fuck!" I panted. That shit looked sexy as fuck.

That shit turned me on to no end. Charlene eyed me seductively and then closed her mouth and swallowed every last bit of my cum. "Oh my God!" I huffed. I couldn't believe my eyes. I immediately thought Leon was the dumbest fuck around to let go of a woman who would do that shit. Most men only dreamed about their wives swallowing. Shit, I literally knew a brother who would sell his left nut to have a woman like that.

Charlene used the back of her hand to wipe her mouth. She looked at me with a real serious look on her face that was kind of scary. "Yeah, that just sealed our deal. Don't fuck around and don't try to fuck me over. You won't like the end result if you do," she told me in a serious and dangerous tone. She didn't give me time to answer her before she was urging me up off the couch.

"Now, come on, let's go. I have two or three more privates tonight," she demanded matter-of-factly, like nothing had just transpired between us.

"No, wait," I said pleadingly. My hands were still shaking from that explosive nut I had just busted. I finally dug into my pocket and pulled out a wad of cash I had just got from the ATM. I wanted Charlene to know that I was dead-ass serious about this plan.

Earlier today, I had cleaned out all of my bank accounts and changed banks, and then I canceled charge cards in both Trice's and my name. I made sure that bitch Trice wouldn't have shit to spend. I saw where she'd taken a hundred dollars out of my fucking account to put on Leon's books, just like Charlene had said.

Fool me once, shame on you. Fool me twice, shame on me.

Try to fool me twice, I would kill that bitch with my bare hands.

Charlene watched me like a hungry dog as I peeled off five one-hundred-dollar bills and handed them to her. "This is the down payment on the job. You find the person and set everything up. Take this and go home for the night. You don't have to do any more privates," I told her.

Charlene snatched the money from my hands so fast I didn't even have a chance to blink. She shuffled the bills and counted them, and then she smiled.

"Trice really don't know what kind of man she is letting go. But then again, no-good bitches never know when they have a good man until he's gone," Charlene stated.

"Or until their asses are gone," I said. We both smiled.

Our deal had definitely been sealed.

12

Leon

By the time I was released back into general population, it seemed like an eternity. My hair had grown inches. I had a beard from not being allowed to shave, and my arms were like monster trucks from all of the push-ups I had been doing to keep myself sane. I was also feeling straight-up crazy from being locked up twenty-three hours a day with one hour out of the hole into a four-by-four cage with the top open.

There were no phone call privileges, no commissary visits, no letters, and no books. Fuck, no nothing.

When they put a motherfucker in the hole, they meant for that shit to be punishment like hell. I was served with my formal re-arrest charges.

Those bastard-ass COs said they had found heroin in two balloons and two razors. They charged me with possession of an illegal substance, which tacked on six more months to my sentence, and then the weapons charges totaled another six months. I went ballistic when they told me they'd added a year to my bid.

I had to be restrained once again by at least ten COs. One of the COs suffered a broken ankle in the fracas, so that earned me some more time in the hole, but no more on my overall sentence. *Thank you for small favors.*

I was fucked up in the game, to say the least. Today, I would finally see the light of day. I guess the warden decided it was time to release one of his caged animals back into the wild. When the COs came to release me from the hole this time, I was calm as a motherfucker. I didn't want anything to keep me from getting the hell out of there. I was itching to get back on the yard so I could see that nigga Kenny. I had done nothing during my time in solitary confinement but think about how I was going to murk that nigga as soon as I see his ass.

I was reissued a new set of prison jumpers and a pair of white prison sneaks. I was also given a new bed bundle that consisted of a hard-ass wool blanket, a thin-ass mattress roll, a flimsy pillow, and some watered down prison toiletries. The COs led me to D block. I had previously been housed in C block, which was much calmer. D block had a reputation for being rough and dangerous, because it housed some of the prison's more problem inmates.

It was all good. I knew how to handle myself just fine.

I walked onto my new cellblock as if I owned that shit. Showing any fear or apprehension was a sure way to get your ass fucked up behind the walls. I could feel the heat of niggas' eyes on me as I passed them to get to my cell and bunk. But I didn't let that shit deter my swagger.

I was walking with the confidence of a lion in the jungle. Like I was the motherfucking lion king. I got into my cell and my new celly was already inside. He had the bottom bunk occupied, just as I thought he would. Only the new cats get the top bunk, which was fucked up for me. Being on the top bunk made you much more vulnerable to a sneak attack. The bottom bunk provided a much better view of niggas rolling up on you. Little shit like that made a big difference in prison.

I sucked my teeth when I saw my celly chilling on the bunk I wanted. I reluctantly threw my shit on the top bunk and started carving out a place for myself in the small-ass cell. I purposely pushed his shit aside on the little cinder-block wall shelf. I did it to prove a point, but the man didn't even budge. He kept right on reading whatever it was he was reading. I figured I would get territorial again. This time, I picked up a stack of books he had on the floor and threw them across the cell so I could put my shit down.

The man finally looked up from his book. His face was stony and serious. "Those are holy books and should be treated as such. I implore you to pick them up and return them to a nice, neat stack and show some reverence . . . my brother," he said calmly, but never changed his rock-hard glare.

I let out a puff of breath from my mouth. "What, nigga? I ain't picking up shit. Those shits ain't no holy books to me. Fuck you and your books." I was being tough, but my stomach was in knots. This was a territory battle, but I didn't know what to expect from him.

"My brother, have some respect. I am calling on the God in you to pick up my holy books and place them in a respectable manner," he said again.

This time I was determined to prove my point. "Yo, you must don't speak English," I retorted. Then I walked over to where the books had landed and kicked them shits. I heard some pages rip as a result. "Now, I said I don't give a fuck about your books."

I made the cardinal mistake you could make in prison. After I kicked the shit out of the books, I turned my back and continued to do my thing. The next thing I felt was a strong force pulling me down. Then I began to gag. The man had got up so quietly and swiftly that I didn't even realize he'd moved. He used his forearm to put me into a sleeper hold. I was no match for him after he lifted me off my feet. My legs dangled like a lifeless rag doll and I could feel the walls closing in on me. Blackness started to cloud the edges of my eyes and suddenly, involuntary sleep overcame me.

I don't know how long I was blacked out. When I came to, I was on the floor of the cell with all of those fucking books sitting on my chest. I moved and it felt like my head was going to explode. I lifted my hand to my forehead and felt blood. Damn, that dude must've just let my ass fall flat when I blacked out. I moved the books and struggled to sit up. With the way I felt, I couldn't get feisty with that dude even if I wanted to.

"I'm Brother Mustafa. Welcome to D block. You can put those books away when you're ready," the dude said calmly as he watched me slip down twice as I tried in vain to get up.

"What the fuck, man?" I winced.

"I asked you nicely, but I guess you wanted to prove a point. I do not believe in violence, but I will do anything to protect what I feel strongly about . . . and my Qurans are the few things I would kill for," Brother Mustafa explained.

I finally stood up. I felt slightly wobbly, but I was able to put his books back. And I immediately realized that being in D block might not be as bad as I thought, especially if I could get a nigga like Brother Mustafa on my team when it came time for me to get Kenny's ass.

13

Trice

I had been trying to be nice to Troy since our little confrontation. But nothing worked. I had even tried to give him some ass, but he had rejected my advances. I was starting to feel hopeless and helpless. Troy had been leaving the house late at night after he came home from work. I was too afraid to ask him where he was going. I thought if I did, he would react the way he had the day I came back from visiting Leon. I had never seen Troy get angry and certainly had never experienced him putting his hands on me in any kind of way.

I couldn't afford to lose him now, especially with the baby's arrival only three weeks away. I had no place else to turn. I hadn't even heard from Leon since the visit, and I was too afraid that if I tried to visit him, Troy would do something crazy like follow me and find out.

I did, however, manage to send Leon a letter letting him know what had happened. I told him to write me back and send the letter to my sister's house. But I still hadn't received shit from him.

I sat at the kitchen table with my head in my hands. I had been sick with worry over the situation. I heard Troy come into the kitchen, and I lifted up my head. He didn't even acknowledge my presence. I felt a deep sinking feeling inside. I watched as he moved around, making himself breakfast. He used to wait on me hand and foot. Now I couldn't even get a simple "good morning" or eye contact from my own husband.

I looked at my watch. It was getting close to the time we needed to head out. It was our first doctor's appointment since our fight.

"Troy, are you going to be ready to leave soon?" I asked in the softest voice I could muster up. He didn't even bother to turn toward me or anything.

"Go by yourself," he said flatly.

I actually felt a sharp pain in my heart when those words left his mouth. He had never, ever let me go to a prenatal appointment alone. He was way too excited about the baby, and he was usually the first one up and ready when he knew we had an appointment.

"What did you say?" I asked for clarification. I could feel a lump in my throat.

"You fucking heard me, Trice! Go by your fucking self to the doctor! I am not interested!" Troy turned toward me as if he was going to attack me again. I flinched and the tears immediately sprang to my eyes.

"Troy! Why are you doing all of this? Please stop!" I cried out.

"I suggest you get the fuck away from me, Trice. I don't want to see you or that baby. I don't want to know anything about your fucking baby!" he growled in a low, deep, eerie voice. The sound of his voice made me shiver.

"Oh my God! I can't believe you're doing this!" I said.

I covered my mouth with my hand and shot up out of the chair. I got up so fast the chair went slamming to the tiled floor. I almost slipped as I raced out of the kitchen, walking as fast as my swollen feet would allow me to go. I was in shock and disbelief. I decided right then that Troy must've known something, and a cold feeling came over me.

Once I was alone in the living room, I stopped moving for a minute. I stood there in one spot with my chest heaving up and down. It was as if my world were spinning off its axis. The perfect little life I envisioned was falling apart at the seams. I was hyperventilating. I couldn't control my sobbing. My makeup was a mess and sweat formed on my forehead.

What have I done? What have I done? I repeated in my head as the tears came down my face like a deluge.

I heard Troy shuffling in the kitchen, and I quickly wobbled toward the door. I knew I was in no condition to drive myself to the doctor's office, but I definitely had to leave the house. Troy had hurt me even worse this time than when he tried to choke me to death.

At that moment, thinking about raising a baby alone with no father, no job, and no resources made me physically sick.

I wasn't one of those women who wanted to be a single mom. I didn't want to do this shit alone. Fuck the superwoman shit. Additionally, if Troy proved it wasn't his baby, how in the hell could I count on Leon when his ass was locked up and couldn't even take care of the son he already had?

I wish I was dead.

14

Charlene

When I answered my house phone and heard the recording from the prison, I almost dropped it to the floor. I squinted my eyes into evil little slits at the thought of Leon calling me now that he was out of the hole. My contacts at the prison told me about his little stint in the hole for having drugs and weapons in his cell. He was actually lucky his ass was in solitary confinement when I sent word to my cousins to have his ass beat the fuck down for what he had done to me. I had since calmed down. I had money on my mind right now, and I wasn't going to let Leon get in the way of that shit.

"Hello," I answered, my voice dry as hell.

"Charlene, it's me. You ain't hear from me because I been in the hole on some trumped-up-ass charges," Leon began. I sighed loudly and rolled my eyes. He went on trying to explain his absence, but I cut his ass right off. I didn't have time for the small-talk bullshit today.

"I know where you been, nigga, and I wasn't thinking about you," I snapped. Leon made a little noise like my response shocked him or something. "In fact, I needed a break from running my ass up there anyway. So what makes you think I even missed your sorry-ass phone calls or visits?"

Leon was quiet for a moment. "What's up with all of that bass in your voice, Charlene?" he had the nerve to ask me.

"Oh, you don't know," I retorted.

"Look, I ain't got time for all of your attitude today. What's up with a visit?" Leon replied as if I hadn't said anything. I pulled the phone away from my ear and looked at it like I hadn't heard his ass correctly.

"What? I ain't never visiting your ass again, nigga. Matter of fact, why don't you let your new baby mama put money on your books and come up there for them conjugal visits, too, you piece of shit!" I screamed at his ass. I could hear Leon sucking his teeth, and I knew the script flip was about to come. Whenever he got caught, he tried to turn it around to where he was the one on the giving end of the screaming.

"What the fuck is you talking about, Charlene? You been fucking smoking again?" Leon barked into the phone.

"Don't even try to deny it, Leon! I saw the visitor log, and I know that bitch Trice has been up there more than once! I also happen to know that she is pregnant with your fucking baby!" I screeched at the top of my lungs.

"Charlene—" Leon tried to get a word in edgewise. I wasn't even fucking having it.

"Don't call my fucking name. I know all the shit that's been going down with y'all trifling asses. But guess what? Her fucking husband also knows, and that bitch been round there sucking the skin off his dick so he won't leave her dumb ass. That serves you and her right. She gon' be right in her little house on the fucking prairie raising your baby with the next man. Meanwhile, you ain't never going to see your son again, and I'd be a dead bitch if I ever come to see your black ass again.

"Oh, yeah, you dumb fuck, I hope you didn't think she was going to stand by your trifling jailbird ass. You and Troy both thought that bitch was wife extraordinaire . . . I guess that bitch showed y'all she ain't nothing but a ho extraordinaire! Now lose my motherfucking number!"

"What, bitch? You don't know shit—"

I didn't give Leon a chance to get his words out. I hung up on his ass. I was no longer going to stand for his out and out disrespect whenever he so pleased. Let Trice's ass be his punching bag from now on. If she didn't visit or write or send his ass money, I didn't know who would, because it sure wasn't going to be me.

It felt real good and empowering to bang that fucking phone on Leon's ass. He had done so many disrespectful things to me, but it sure felt good to give the shit back to him. It was something I had never had the courage to do before. Even when he was just an outright dirty dog to me, I had never really given up on him. But things had changed drastically. I was going to get myself and my son out of the hood, but not before all of these people who ruined my life— Leon, Trice, and even Troy—felt my wrath.

Leon called back six times before he finally gave up. I guess the dudes in the phone line weren't having that shit anymore. Each time he called, I would just not accept the call and hang the fuck up. I planned on calling Verizon to have them block collect calls from the correctional facility. That would teach Leon's ass a lesson or two or three. Fucking with Charlene would get your ass hurt in more ways than one.

I got myself focused on the business at hand. I picked up my cell and called Troy to meet me at the club again tonight. I explained to him the importance of his presence and he agreed to be there. He had been meeting me at least twice a week since our first meeting.

Tonight was going to be different, though.

This was the meeting that I would tell him

what the *hit man* was going to charge and how everything was going to go down with the plan. The guy wanted me to make sure Troy wasn't playing any games before he agreed to do the hit. I wanted to look Troy in the eyes and see if he was dead serious or had just been talking out of his ass, because he was angry at the time.

After my and Troy's initial meeting, where he told me he wanted to put a hit out on Trice for insurance money, it hadn't taken me no time to set everything up. Especially after Troy threw that million-dollar number out there. My connection was only charging Troy twenty thousand for the hit, but I was going to tell Troy tonight that the hit was forty thousand up front.

I could see the dollar signs now.

I had to make sure I was taken care of, and that up-front money was guaranteed money . . . money in hand. The insurance money was going to take some time to come through. Knowing insurance companies, it would take some time to conduct an investigation to make sure whatever happened to Trice was an accidental death or death by natural cause. With all of that going on, the dough would definitely help me pay my damn bills for a few months without showing my face back up at the Glass Slipper. I had plans on quitting the club as soon as the hit was set up. I guess I could've just explained my position to Troy. I was sure he would've understood all of that. But I still wasn't going to tell him that I was about to rob his ass by doubling the hit man's number.

Believe it or not, I had actually begun to look forward to my meetings with Troy. We had also taken our sexual tension a few steps further after the second or third meeting in the club's champagne room. Troy paid well too. He had this thing about me having to do privates with other men. On any night Troy came to the club, he would fork over a few hundred dollars and tell me I could quit for the night. Of course, I never did and as soon as Troy left, I was on to the next.

Our meetings finally escalated to all-out fucking. The club didn't have the same rules as some of the other establishments in Virginia Beach. I had to admit, Troy's dick was pretty damn small, but I knew how to work my hips enough to make myself get off and get him off too. Just thinking about old boring-ass Trice and her stuck-up self, I couldn't see how she and Troy had ever had a successful sex life. I mean, damn, both people can't be boring and dry and then add in Troy's small-ass dick and that shit just made me shudder.

Troy was definitely no Leon in bed. Trice probably got a taste of Leon's big, fantastic dick and lost her damn mind. No wonder she was ready to throw away her little white-picket fence life to be with Leon—that bitch was dick-whipped.

Well, I'd rather have a pocket full of dough than some convict nigga with a big dick.

I waited until Troy arrived at our usual meeting time, and then I came from the dressing room downstairs. I knew if I had come up any earlier, somebody would've grabbed me and I would've been occupied when Troy got there. That happened a few times and he had gotten a little upset. I even had to set him straight and remind him that I was not his wife, girlfriend, jump-off, or nothing of the sort, so if he got to the club and I was working, his ass would have to wait. But tonight I couldn't afford to ruffle any of Troy's feathers. Not when I was so close to getting hold of some good money from his simple ass.

"Hey, Charlene," Troy greeted me. He didn't smile this time, and he seemed super nervous. He had his hat pulled super low, and his hands were shoved deep down in his coat pockets. I mean, Troy just looked like he was up to no fucking good. I looked him up and down good, and a strange feeling came over me.

"Why you look so leery?" I asked him. My tone suggested that I was annoyed. Weak men made me sick, and I was thinking Troy better not have come to tell me he was having cold fucking feet. That is how shook up he was acting.

"I'm fine. I just had a long day. Trice and I are not doing good right now . . . you should understand," Troy told me.

We started walking and I rolled my eyes without him seeing me. Did he really think I gave a flying fuck about the problems he was having with his cheating-ass wife? Sometimes Troy didn't display one stitch of common sense. Fuck! He was about to kill the bitch for insurance money and he was worried about them not doing good. Really?

"Please! It's been weeks. You should be over that bitch. Don't be having no second thoughts, Troy, because I already have my guy all ready to roll on this thing," I grumbled as we entered our regular room.

"Charlene, I don't want to have sex or anything tonight. I just want to discuss what we need to discuss and get back home. I'm really tired."

That surprised me. "Well, excuse me!" I snapped. Here I was neglecting my other clients for his ass and he had the nerve to be cutting me short. I was expecting his money, so I hadn't made one dime yet.

"I'm sorry, but I just need to get things in motion before I have second thoughts," Troy said.

I folded my face into a scowl. "Didn't I fucking know you were going to have second thoughts, Troy," I whispered harshly. I couldn't take a chance with my voice getting picked up by the security cameras. Troy put his hands up in surrender.

"I'm not having second thoughts! It's just been too long, and I need some assurances that this is going to go through!" he shot back. Yeah, something was definitely up with Troy tonight. He very rarely raised his voice at me.

"Okay, you want it to be all business, then that's how I'll carry it. I spoke to my guy. He wants fifty thousand up front," I told Troy. That's right—I added another ten thousand dollars because I didn't fucking like Troy's attitude or tone of voice.

"What? Where am I supposed to get that kind of money from up front?" Troy barked.

"Shhh! Shut the fuck up before you let all your dumb-ass business out into the street."

Troy put his head into his hands like the sorry little wimpy ass he was. I should've realized he would never, ever man the fuck up.

"Okay . . . okay. When does he want to get the first half of the payment?" Troy whispered.

"First half? Nah, he don't work like that. He ain't no fucking bill collector. He wants it all up front and then he'll do the deed." I was looking at the nigga like he had lost his mind. "I know you ain't street smart, but niggas don't do murders on consignment and shit," I said in Troy's ear.

He looked up and rubbed his chin. "Give me a week. I'll have to get the money from a few different places," Troy informed me.

"I hope he is still around and willing to do it in a week," I said slickly. Shit, I wanted the money. Fuck what Troy was trying to talk about.

All these weeks he had already been waiting for the insurance policy grace period to be over, you mean to tell me he didn't get his chips up for the hit? "I mean, did you think this shit was going to be done for free?" I asked him irritably.

"No, but I thought it would be a reasonable price like ten thousand," Troy whispered harshly.

"Well, your ass apparently thought wrong. Just call me and let me know what you want to do," I said snidely.

"I want to meet the guy." Troy came out of nowhere with that request.

My heart started racing like crazy. "Um . . . I . . . I told you, he don't let nobody know who he is. He is too leery of the cops or a setup," I stammered, but recovered quickly.

"I need some proof that this is all legit before I just hand over that kind of money, Charlene," Troy gritted. This dude was getting real funky with me all of a sudden.

"I'll see what he says, but I can't guarantee nothing," I told him.

"Try your best or I might have to look elsewhere," Troy said. He stood up and headed for the door. Troy left me sitting there fuming and nervous, all at the same time. My gut was telling me that something about Troy's behavior just wasn't right.

I was frantic when I left the champagne room. I was still broke after being at the club all night, and now I had to show Troy a face. My mind raced a million miles a minute. I was starting to see what was once a perfect plan fall apart right in front of my eyes. "Shit, Charlene! Think, bitch, think!" I cursed to myself under my breath as I stomped toward the door to the club's basement. Someone grabbed my arm and broke my train of thought.

"Aye, girl, where you been?" I heard the voice and I immediately wanted to throw up. But suddenly an idea hit me over the head like an anvil in a cartoon. I plastered on a fake-ass smile and turned around innocently.

"Joe, my favorite guy! How you been, baby? Long time, no see. You know big mama missed all of this," I said seductively, rubbing his nasty-ass protruding gut.

Joe started laughing excitedly and his midsection began jiggling. I wanted to cut my own hand off rather than touch that shit. His shirt was all wet with sweat too.

"I been missing you, girl. I been dreaming of this fat ass and those juicy titties," Joe replied, rubbing his rough, calloused hands over my ass. Oh God, you have no idea how much I wanted to just throw up and run.

"Oooh, boy, you know I missed your ass. I been so sad without you," I lied like a motherfucker. But it was what I needed to do. "So what you doing here? You came to see little ol' me or you want another girl?" I asked, playing the fool.

"C'mon now, you know Joe only got eyes for your pretty chocolate-dipped ass," he replied.

Gag me with a spoon. "So what can I do for you, baby? You here for a private tonight?" I cooed. I should've earned the top acting award for this performance, that was for damn sure.

"You know it, girl. Take me to the back and show your daddy what that fine ass working with this evening," Joe replied. This time he slapped me on the ass so hard, it stung like a bitch. I bit down hard and told myself I had to take it. I had something in mind the minute I saw Joe.

"Oooh, you into the slapping thing tonight, are you?" I giggled. Inside I was burning mad. Joe followed me to one of the back rooms. He was breathing all hard from the walk. I said a silent prayer that God would just help me get through this private. Joe was talking mad reckless shit all the way to the room. I kept giggling like a schoolgirl and egging him on. He just didn't know that I had a bigger and better plan for his three-hundred-pound smelly ass.

Just grin and bear it, Charlene. Just grin and bear it, I chanted inside of my head.

Joe was going to be a hit man. *He just didn't know it yet.*

15

Troy

I left the Glass Slipper feeling worse than ever before. I didn't know what I had been thinking, but I guess I was starting to come to my senses. I was having second thoughts about killing Trice, and involving Charlene had been the worst mistake of my life. My judgment had been clouded by anger over Trice's betrayal and Charlene's sex. Now I was in way too deep, because the guy Charlene had set everything up with was not going to turn back now.

My mind raced a million miles a minute as I drove toward my home. I got off the highway and pulled my car over. I couldn't help the tears that were falling from my eyes. When I thought back over everything that had happened from the day I convinced Trice to participate in the *Trading Spouses* show to the day I found out she had fucked Leon to the baby not being mine, I just felt like killing myself and not Trice.

"It's all your fucking fault!" I screamed, and slammed my fists on the steering wheel. "You did this to your marriage and to Trice!" I yelled at myself repeatedly. My hands were curled into fists, and I could feel the vein in my neck pulsing. I had never had this kind of anger until now. I was a man on the verge of destruction. I bent down and reached into my glove box. I pulled out the small .22 caliber pistol I kept in there. I held the gun in my hand for a few minutes and then I put it to my temple.

"Yeah, you need to just end this shit now. It's all your fault anyway," I mumbled through clenched teeth. I could hear cars whipping past me on the highway. That's how I deserved to die . . . right there with a gun to my head. I closed my eyes and slipped my finger through the trigger guard. "Don't be a bitch all of your life, Troy! You can't even man up enough to put yourself out of your own misery."

I was shaking all over now. I didn't think I had ever felt that level of fear in my entire life. I started pulling back on the trigger slowly. I was breathing rapidly, the breath coming out of my mouth in strong puffs. I needed to build the courage to just end it all now. The trigger was coming back, and I was waiting to feel the blast to my head at any second now.

Then, *bang, bang, bang*! "Aye! Drop the weapon! Drop the fucking weapon!"

I jumped and dropped the gun just before the trigger went back enough to send a blast into my brains. I dropped the weapon and threw my hands in the air. When I turned, there were about five state troopers surrounding my car. The door flung open and I was dragged out of the car.

"I'm not trying to hurt nobody, Officer. I was going to kill myself," I said as I was thrown face-down into the dirt.

"Somebody called in a man with a gun on the side of the highway. What the fuck are you doing out here, boy?" the redneck state trooper drawled in his Southern accent.

"I don't know. I don't even know," I mumbled as I was hoisted up and thrown into the back of a police vehicle.

I was hauled down to the police station. All eyes were on me when I got there. I guess the call had come through that a crazy man had a gun to his head on the side of the highway. I was placed in a room, but I wasn't handcuffed. Maybe I wasn't under arrest? Committing suicide wasn't a crime. The gun wasn't mine, though. That might render a problem. I sat with my head in my hands for what seemed like an eternity. This was a snag in the program that I couldn't afford to have happen. Two officers came into the room after a while.

"Son, I am Officer Bradley and this here is Officer Cooley," a tall, pale-faced, big-bellied officer announced.

I just rolled my eyes at them both.

"Now, tell us why you were on the side of a highway with a gun to your head . . . a gun that ain't registered to you at all," the officer asked and told me at the same time.

"I'm . . . mmm . . . sorry, Officer. I just have a lot going on at home. It won't happen again if you just let me out of here. My wife . . . she's . . . she's pregnant," I managed to say.

My emotions were betraying me and getting the best of me again, and I started the crying shit. I started to think about Trice and the baby being dead. I started to think about how the fuck I was going to get fifty thousand dollars to Charlene's dude and if I didn't what a street nigga might do to me. It was all just too much; that's why my ass was on the side of the highway. I didn't tell the cops that, though.

"You been drinking, son?" Officer Bradley asked.

I looked at the table just in time to see them slide the Breathalyzer over toward me.

"I haven't, sir. I told you I just had a lapse in judgment for a minute. I promise, if you just let me out of here, it won't happen again," I pleaded.

The officers looked at each other.

"We found some things during our inventory of your car. Considering the situation, it was legal for us to inventory the car. . . . We want to talk to you about some of the stuff we found," Officer Cooley said. He had a funny look on his face.

I immediately got anxious. I couldn't think straight about what I had in the car. I knew I had just met up with Charlene to discuss stuff, but she didn't give me anything or did she? I couldn't remember.

"Son . . . you better start talking. We want to know more about this," Officer Bradley drawled as he slid some papers toward me. I looked down and started to cry again.

"I can explain it all," I finally relented. There was nothing else I could do at that point, except go along with whatever they wanted me to tell them.

16

Leon

That bitch Charlene had pissed me off so bad I almost went back to my cellblock and got into some shit with the other inmates. She had me fed for real. She had cursed me out on the first phone call I had made to her in weeks. The nerve of her ass. Then she made it worse when she told me not to ever call her again or expect any visits. But what pissed me off the most was when she told me that I would never lay eyes on my son again. That was some shit that might make the average nigga happy, but my son was my world. Being locked up and not seeing him was hard enough, but to think Charlene would purposely keep him away from me was enough to make me want to take her apart limb by limb.

She kind of shocked me when she told me she had found out Trice was visiting with me and that the baby Trice was carrying was mine. Obviously I had underestimated Charlene. I never gave her enough smart credit to think she would ever uncover my scheme with her and Trice. Initially, I couldn't believe Charlene was intelligent or sophisticated enough to put two and two together.

I wracked my brain trying to figure out how that could have happened. It all boiled down to that sneaky bitch telling me she wasn't coming for a visit, but then she showed up for her regular Saturday visit. I guess she couldn't get in and—*boom!*—she found out Trice was here. That shit blew my mind, though. I thought those two would never cross paths, and I had been extra careful making sure I scheduled their visits so there was no conflict.

It fucked me up when I lost my connection with Charlene. Damn, she was my fail-safe, the only person out in the world who would be there through anything. She kept my books on pile and she provided me essentials like socks, T-shirts, underwear, and anything the prison allowed me to have. I was in love with Trice and with the idea of having a woman like her, but I had to face it—she wasn't street smart, and she really wasn't built to ride a bid with a nigga. Trice was all right and shit, except for the fact that she was still living with Troy like they were a happy little couple. That shit burned me up inside.

Trice also didn't have her own paper. Anytime I asked her to do anything for me, she had to beg, borrow, or steal from Troy. That shit wasn't cool at all. It was now a fucked-up situation, and I might end up without either one of them supporting or standing behind me.

Two days after my explosive phone call with Charlene, I received my mail from the COs and saw that she had sent me a letter. I opened the shit thinking it would be her telling me she was sorry and that she was wrong and asking if we could work things out. That was what she usually did, even if I was wrong. I was shocked as shit when I finally climbed up on my bunk and read Charlene's letter. This chick was telling me all about how she had fucked Troy and how it was. I read the lines Charlene wrote over and over again:

> *Oh yeah, and just so you know. Revenge is a motherfucker. I fuck Troy almost every day now. He is lying in my bed as I write this letter. I guess you can get pussy from Trice when you marry her. Oh wait, she ain't leaving Troy yet.*
>
> *You know what he told me? That he also fucks Trice every night. I couldn't care less. Troy is spending time with your son and filling in for you too. I guess when Trice's baby comes, he'll be*

doing the same on that end. I guess he takes your status as pimp. You had both of us and now Troy has both of us. I guess the fool turns out to be you. Bitch-ass nigga.

She knew just what to write to get under my skin. If it was one thing that Charlene had learned to do over the course of our fucked-up marriage, it was how to make me angry enough to want to kill a motherfucker. I read that shit so many times I thought I actually started hearing Charlene's ghetto, bird-ass voice actually saying the words to me. I could picture her with her shiny-ass hair weave that didn't even look real, with her black-ass face twisted and her head cocked to the side telling me that she was fucking my former best friend.

The fucked-up thing was I believed every word of that fucking letter. Charlene was a liar in her own right, but with something like that, I believed that Charlene and Troy were that fucking foul to hook up just to get back at me.

I couldn't front, her letter and the shit she said in it had my insides on boil and I was raging fucking mad. My manhood had been tested by my fucking wife! Charlene also said in the letter that there were pictures of her and Troy getting it on, but I guess the COs who monitored the mail at the prison took the pictures out before I could see them. I think seeing those pictures would've definitely made me catch wreck on any random nigga in D block, which of course, would've sent my ass packing right back to the hole.

After reading that letter, I crumpled that shit up into a little ball and threw it across the cell. I bit down into my bottom lip so hard, I drew blood. The metallic taste of it made me feel animalistic and I wanted to wreak havoc on someone. I wasn't trying to punch no walls this time. Shit, last time I did that I ended up in a cast, which was no joke in solitary.

"You better hope I never see your ass again, bitch," I mumbled to myself as if Charlene could hear me. I had never felt such a strong sense of powerlessness in my entire life. I didn't even feel this powerless when my step-pops used to bust my mother's ass and I was too young to do anything about it. And that was some devastating shit. But to me, this shit was even worse.

I knew I would crumple Charlene's ass just like that letter if I ever saw her again. Most people would say I was wrong for being mad at her since I had done her dirty. But I didn't see shit like most people. Charlene knew the deal, and she got what the fuck her hand called for. She should've left me the first time I cheated. By staying, all she did was tell me I had free rein to do me. I guess this was her little revenge trip. It would be all good, unless, of course, I got out early and went to see her ass.

If I hadn't spoken to Trice right after reading

the letter and found out that she wasn't still fucking Troy, I might've felt that all hope was lost. When I spoke to her, she told me it didn't make a difference what Troy threatened to do to her, she couldn't resist coming to see me. Trice's impending visit was probably the only thing that kept me from flipping and earning myself another stint in the hole.

Sure enough, just like she said, Trice showed up to the Tuesday visit. I was happy as hell to see that she had kept her word and come to visit. I tried to play it cool, but I was both nervous and relieved as hell to see her pretty ass sitting there in front of me. I prayed all the way to the table that things were going to be all right between us. But for some reason, something was eating at me. I had a feeling something just wasn't right.

As soon as I sat down in front of Trice, my heart sank into the pit of my stomach. I could tell by her facial expression that Trice was stressed the fuck out. Her face said everything. It was as if the life had been sucked out of her. She wasn't her usual beautiful perky self. Her eyes were all puffy and dark underneath. It was scary-looking, kind of zombielike. I could tell she wasn't getting any sleep. I examined her some more as we sat in silence for a few minutes. Trice's face wasn't glowing like it usually did, and she had her hair pulled back into a sloppy ponytail. I had never seen her wear a ponytail. She was way too classy for that. This wasn't the woman I knew; this wasn't like Trice at all. She had never come on a visit with nothing less than a perfectly made up face, newly done hairdo, and a big bright smile.

I honestly felt horrible for her. I also felt a tad bit responsible. In a way, I put her in this position. I didn't know why, but I just wanted to reach out and grab her for a big hug and kiss. I knew it wasn't permitted, so I kept my cool. Spending time in the hole changed your perspective on a lot of things. Once you were identified as a disciplinary problem, you were one write-up from the hole again. As much as I wanted to hug Trice, I had to refrain.

"What's up, baby girl?" I asked softly as I stared her down. Trice closed her eyes and immediately started to cry. That shit actually broke my heart. I knew I could be real selfish, but not to this extent. "Shhh, what's going on?" I asked. I was pretty sure I knew why she was stressed out. If Charlene knew about Trice visiting me, there was no doubt in my mind that she had probably run her fucking blabbermouth and told Troy.

Trice looked at me pitifully. Her bottom lip quivered like crazy. "Leon, I came to tell you in person that I won't be back to visit. I have to do what is right for the baby, and I'm trying to work things out with Troy," Trice said, stifling her tears. I could tell she was trying to be strong, but what about me? In light of that news, how in the fuck was I supposed to feel? She had dropped a fucking bomb on me like never before. I sat back in the hard visitors' room chair and glared across the table at her. I couldn't help but be overcome with anger and hurt.

"You fucking lied to me?" I exploded. "You told me you couldn't resist coming to see me!"

"No, Leon, I actually came here to tell you that I'm not going to continue seeing you," Trice answered, her voice still quivering. It was as if she had slapped me in the face. I would've never expected a bold-face fucking lie from Trice like this. She just wanted to visit me to break this fucking bad news to me. That was some cold-ass shit.

"Nah . . . don't come here to tell me that bullshit! You could've said that dumb shit on the phone and saved us both the fucking trouble! You better fucking remember that you are carrying my fucking baby! I'm not having it, Trice! You will visit me!"

Trice seemed shocked and startled by my outburst. The bass in my voice garnered disapproving looks from the COs, so I quickly tried in vain to tone it down. "Trice, you love me . . . not that nigga Troy, remember? You were the one who reached out to me when I got locked up. I didn't ask you to come and start this shit," I leaned into the table and whispered harshly. "You started visiting me. You were the one who said you couldn't resist seeing me, being with me, and that it was my baby you are carrying. I put my fucking marriage on the line for you, even though you were still living with my fucking best friend." My nostrils were flaring like a bull seeing red. My hands were curled into fists, and I balled up my toes in my shoes. It was all I could do to keep my cool in that room full of people. I didn't know how long that shit would last, though.

"I know all of that, Leon, but Troy is a provider. I can't take any more chances coming here. He knows something is up and he has been different toward me. I think he is starting to figure out that I am doing something shady. He has taken away access to *our* money. I'm totally at his mercy right now. What if he throws me out with the baby? Where will I go? To my sister? She can't even manage with her kids in her little place.

"Troy provides me with a good home, Leon. I'm sorry, I just can't throw that away for you, and you are locked up right now. Maybe you should just try to mend your relationship with Charlene, and we should all go back to the way things were before the spouse trade." The tears fell through her words.

I was glaring at her. I could feel the fire rising inside my chest. I could barely control my breathing at that moment. I could actually see myself putting my hands around Trice's neck and squeezing until she lost consciousness . . . *until she was holding on to dear life.*

I guess she could sense my extreme anger. The look on her face said it all. Trice stood up from the chair and looked down at me with sorrowful eyes, like I was a fucking charity case. Just that look on her face told me she felt sorry for me, as if I were less than a man to her at that moment. For the first time since I had been arrested, she made me feel like I was a . . . convict.

"I'm sorry, Leon. I have to go. There is nothing else left for us," she said, and just like fucking that, she turned her back on me.

I began banging my fists on the table like a madman. I watched Trice walk away with pure evil in my heart. I wanted to jump up and run after her. Part of me wanted to go after her and kiss her. But the other part of me wanted to run after her and beat her until she bled.

This bitch had helped to ruin my life with Charlene, and now she was putting the pieces of her shit back together. Whether I loved her or not, she was a lying bitch.

"Work things out with Charlene? You fucked that up! I can't work things out with Charlene and I ain't got nobody else! You fucking bitch! You just like the rest of these trifling-ass bitches! That nigga Troy gonna know that ain't his baby!" I screamed loudly as Trice wobbled toward the exit.

She was shaking her head and I could tell she was still crying, but she never turned around to look at me. I was still banging on the table and screaming Trice's name. Three COs rushed over and roughly grabbed me out of the chair. The entire visitors' room was watching this whole crazy scene unfold. I didn't care. I didn't give a damn who saw me act the fool. I was watching my entire life flash before my fucking eyes. I think for the first time since my step-pops beat my mom, I felt hurt. The only difference was this hurt was directly inflicted on me, not someone else.

"Get the fuck off me! I ain't got shit to lose now! I will fuck all y'all up! I ain't got shit left to live for now!" I hollered as they roughly dragged me out of the visitors' area. I knew once we were out of sight, those fucking COs were going to beat my ass. I didn't even give a fuck. "I'ma fucking hurt y'all! I ain't got shit left!" I screamed some more.

The last person I saw watching me before I got pulled through the door was Brother Mustafa, my cellmate. He was just staring at me. His facial expression was stoic. I locked eyes with him, and I could see in his eyes that he looked down on me as if I were a crazy person . . . or better yet, an animal.

At that moment, I was a man undone.

I had started out with two women in my corner to ride this bid with me and now I had none.

Shit was about to get critical for me.

17

Trice

I walked out of the visitors' room as fast as my sore legs and fat feet would allow me. Due to my pregnancy, I couldn't move as fast as I would have liked. Still, my legs burned with every step. It felt as if I had two lead pipes attached to me, not to mention the huge weight that sat in my midsection.

The baby was so big now that I couldn't walk regularly, much less speed walk. I had to wobble and that put strain on my back too. My damn body ached all over, but I kept moving. I had to get as far away from Leon and his vituperative tirade as quickly as possible.

I was actually in shock at his outlandish behavior. He had gone completely off the deep end and acted crazy as hell when I told him I wasn't going to be visiting him anymore. Didn't he expect that the news would be coming sooner or later? I mean, he was fucking locked up!

Leon had started down one side and came up the other side with the insults he hurled at me in front of a visitors' room filled with people. I had to just shake my head at some of the things he was yelling at me and some of the names he had called me. Everything happened for a reason, and I guess Leon's blatant disrespect told me what I needed to know about him. It was a good thing I had decided to use my head and decided to stay with Troy to raise my baby with some semblance of stability.

Still, even though I was firm in my decision to stop fucking with Leon, I was a complete emotional wreck by the time I left the visitors' room. Deep down inside, I really did have feelings for Leon. I knew it sounded crazy because of everything that had happened and all of the circumstances surrounding our little tryst, but it was true. I knew right away that I loved Leon. I realized that at some point during the last nine months, and since the trade, my feelings for Leon had gone from lust to some kind of deep, crazy love.

With my feelings overwhelming me to the point I had risked everything I had, I quickly came to the realization that I had never been in love with Troy. I married him out of need and

130

desire for financial stability, not for the feelings he invoked inside of me. Leon had been the first man to actually kindle that fire inside of me. It was a feeling that I never wanted to stop experiencing, but I had to give it up cold turkey. If I didn't, I was sure Troy would catch on and the consequences would be catastrophic . . . for me and the baby.

Today's decision to stop fucking with Leon was hard, but necessary. I was beginning to think Troy had figured me out since I didn't really treat him like a wife should treat a husband. As I made it to the prison's exit doors, I shook my head, trying to clear my muddled mind. It was all too much to think about in my condition.

I stepped outside of the prison and inhaled the fresh outdoor air. It felt so good to my lungs. I guess in the past, being so caught up with seeing Leon, I had never really noticed how stale the air inside the prison could be.

Today, I realized that the inside of the prison was dank and cold, and the air was thick and stale with tension and pain. For the first time, I felt the stifling air as if it were choking the life out of me. The feeling was multiplied by ten, and I actually thought I was suffocating. Maybe the reality that freedom was not promised to anyone was what made me feel claustrophobic today as well.

I whirled around outside, feeling kind of confused and dazed. I leaned up against the building to get my bearings. Leon had really done a number on my nerves.

"Calm down, Trice," I mumbled, placing my hand over my chest to calm myself down. Then I took a minute to inhale and exhale a few more times because I was feeling funny . . . kind of light-headed and dizzy. I moved my hand from my chest down to my abdomen and rubbed my stomach. Tears formed in my eyes again. Reality was a bitch and today I was getting a reality check like never before.

"Shhh," I whispered, rubbing my stomach. I was trying to calm my baby, who was really active inside of me, like she was trying to bust right out. I knew they said a fetus could sense when things weren't right with its mother. I knew that had to be true from the way my unborn baby girl was going crazy. I guess it was because of the drama. Maybe she knew I was going to bring her into this crazy world to live a lie for the rest of her life and mine.

"Get to your car. All you need to do is get to the car. Drive straight home and make the best out of your life," I tried pep talking myself. "Forget about him, Trice. You have a husband and he is willing to take care of you. Forget about him, Trice."

It would take some convincing for me to just completely forget about Leon. I didn't know if I was up for the challenge. I got a lot of stares and glares as I sat on the little shuttle bus that would take me to the prison's parking lot. I wanted to ask some of those ghetto bitches if they had ever seen a pregnant woman crying before! Some of them even had the nerve to whisper about me, just like little project gossip hounds. I turned up my nose at them. I knew they didn't have a life. At least I did have a husband at home. They were all probably riding a bid with some baby daddy who would leave their asses flat and dry when he was released. I was better than them bitches, I told myself. It made me feel better for a few minutes. I still wanted off that little bus.

"Hurry up," I kept saying under my breath. Although the sick feeling I was having was crazy, I shook it off and blamed it on the fact that I had been crying so much after Leon basically went ballistic on me. The little shuttle finally began to pull into the parking lot. It seemed like it had been an eternity, when, in fact, the entire ride took all of five minutes.

By the time it came to a full stop, I felt completely nauseous. I stood up and rolled my eyes at all of the weave-head dumb bitches who had been whispering about me. My legs felt like noodles and I could feel sweat on my forehead. "Ugh," I grunted. I hadn't felt this bad since the beginning of my pregnancy. I was starting to wonder if something was wrong with me or the baby.

As soon as I stepped off the shuttle bus, I doubled over and threw up all over the ground. It had come so hard and so fast that I didn't even have a chance to walk to the side or find a corner of the lot to throw up in.

The CO who drove the shuttle walked to the top of the shuttle's steps and looked down at me with a scowl. "Damn, you couldn't move around the back of the bus and throw up? You threw up right in front of the steps! Now that is just disgusting . . . pregnant or not! How are all these people supposed to get off with your vomit in front of my doors?" he growled insensitively.

I could hear the bitches inside the bus groaning and complaining and cursing too. I was flabbergasted at their complete fucking lack of sympathy. *Didn't pregnancy matter to anyone anymore?* I thought.

I finally stood up straight and that's when I started feeling pain in my lower abdomen. The pains weren't so bad that I couldn't walk, but they were bad enough to alarm me. "Oh God, I have to get to my car. I have to get home to Troy and tell him I don't feel right," I said. No one was listening to me, though. Instead, everybody was glaring at me for being sick. The fucking nerve of these people!

I finally started walking toward my car, but not before I turned toward the shuttle and put up my middle finger at the CO and the other occupants. I could hear them cursing at my back as the CO got ready to pull the shuttle into a different spot so they could all get out without stepping in vomit.

When I sat down in my car, more pain hit me. This time it was stronger than before. I was thinking that pains that come and go must be contractions. "Oww," I moaned. The baby moved some more, this time harder than I had ever felt her move. I was feeling a little bit of pressure down between my legs too.

"Oh, shit, I have to call Troy . . . but where will I tell him I'm at?" I voiced to myself, hoping logic would take over for the damn nerves that were racking me. With shaky hands, I took out my cell phone to call Troy. Of course he didn't answer and my call went to voice mail. That was his usual lately. He had been totally brushing me off, not speaking to me in the house and never taking my phone calls. That shit was pissing me off, especially because in his mind I was supposed to be carrying his fucking baby. I called a few times back-to-back before I decided to finally leave him a message.

"Troy . . . it's Trice. It's an emergency. I think I'm going into labor. Please meet me at home so we can go to the hospital together. I will be home in less than an hour. Please, Troy, we have to do this together," I panted into the phone. It was fucked up because I couldn't even tell him where I was and that it would take me so long to get home. I called my sister and put her on notice that I thought I was in early labor too. She told me to rush my ass home, take a shower, and get my ass to the hospital.

I started my car, put it in gear, and began pulling out of the parking space slowly. More pains rocked through my stomach, which caused me to pause a few times. I was doing my breathing techniques and concentrating on trying to stay calm until I got home. My mind was racing with things I had to do—find Troy, get my hospital bag, get the baby's bag, and call my doctor.

As I mindlessly turned my steering wheel to make the final turn out of the prison's parking lot, I was scared almost half to death when suddenly a black Tahoe with darkly tinted windows came to a screeching halt in front of my car. "Fuck!" I screeched. I almost crashed right into the SUV with the way it just seemed to appear out of nowhere. I slammed on the brakes so hard my body jerked forward. If it wasn't for the seat belt, I would've hit my head on the steering wheel. The seat belt cut into my shoulder and my belly, causing sharp pains in both places. I couldn't fucking believe my eyes!

"Oh my God! What the fuck are you doing?" I screamed, laying on my horn. A man jumped out of the truck and ran toward my car. My eyes popped open with shock. My heart started racing so fast I could feel it in the back of my throat. "What the fuck?" I wolfed. It was happening so fast, I was too shocked to react.

"You're busted, bitch!" the strange man called out as he began lifting something black toward me. I swear to God I could see my life flashing before my eyes. I threw my hands up in defense, but I realized that the man was just snapping pictures of me with a long-lens camera.

"Aggh!" I screamed, throwing my hands up in an attempt to shield my face. It was to no avail. He moved so fast and came around the car several times. The man was relentless in his efforts. He was even so bold as to come to my driver's side window and snap a bunch of close-ups of my face.

"Get the fuck away from my car! Who sent you here? Get out of here!" I screamed at the top of my lungs while I was still trying to shield my face.

The man was laughing as he ran back to the Tahoe. "You fucking bastard!" I screamed, punching my steering wheel. I exhaled and tried to get my nerves to settle. I ran my fingers through my hair and sat there for a few minutes after the Tahoe pulled away. I needed to get my thoughts together in order to be able to drive. Between the pains that were coming and going and now this crazy shit, I was ready to throw in the fucking towel on everything. I knew nobody else had sent the man but Troy. Now he had stooped low enough to have me followed. Ain't that a bitch? Troy was turning into someone I didn't even know.

"I hate you, Troy!" I screamed. I guess the realization that I might really be busted red-handed hit me like a ton of bricks. Just then another thunderbolt of pain rocked through my abdomen. I doubled over and more tears came. My life was over.

I wasn't going to have Leon or Troy. At this rate, I was going to be left with nothing and if that was the case, I was on the receiving end of the same karmic consequence as Leon.

How could I have fucked up my life this badly?

18

Charlene

I took a long pull on my Newport and blew the smoke out hard and fast. I walked around in yet another circle, pacing the floor. I looked at the clock for the hundredth time, which was probably the number of times I had walked in circles. I looked at my cell phone for the thousandth time. Still, no calls or contact from Troy's ass. I told him the last time we met not to fucking play with me. I had a real strong gut feeling that he was going to do some dumb shit, like punk out of our deal. I stubbed out the last cigarette from my pack and tossed the crushed pack onto the floor.

"This is really not fucking cool, Troy! You are playing with me!" I growled to the air. I looked over at my cousin, Dray, and he was staring at me like I was the biggest liar in the fucking world.

"What? He said he would call me! I can't control him!" I snapped, rolling my eyes at Dray. Who the fuck was he to be questioning me anyway? All of this was making me uneasy, especially since I knew the real plan.

I took to pacing again. That motherfucker Troy must've thought I was playing games with his ass. He had not returned my fucking phone calls and it was down to the wire. It was time for me to put the pressure on this nigga. I was fucking angry now. It seemed to me that Troy thought I was one big fat joke that could be used and thrown away. Either he came to the table with the fifty thousand dollars for the hit or I was going to have his ass fucked up by Dray and his boys. That was that.

Dray was down for it from the minute the words had left my mouth. I decided not to get Joe, my fat-ass client, involved. I came to my senses shortly after the thought had hit me. There was no way that soft-ass nigga would've convinced Troy he was a hit man. First, Joe was fat and big and scared of his own shadow. Second, with something like putting a hit on somebody's life, you couldn't be too careful with who to trust, and I already didn't trust a damn soul. Where I grew up, trust was for suckers and fool-ass niggas. I could visualize Joe singing like a bird to the cops if anything went wrong.

After the whole Joe and fake hit man idea went out the window, I thought long and hard and finally decided to really go through with getting a hit man for Troy to have Trice killed. Initially, I was just jerking Troy's chain and acting like I had someone to do the hit on Trice. I didn't have anyone at first, nor was I looking for anyone. My initial plan was to get the up-front payment from Troy and bounce, leaving his ass high and dry and in the dust. I was even going to write Trice an anonymous letter, informing her ass of Troy's plans to kill her. At least she would still be alive to receive the letter. That would've destroyed their marriage just like mine had been destroyed.

I mean, I was a vengeful bitch, but I wasn't actually going to help this nigga kill his wife. That was some foul shit for him to even come up with. I had obviously underestimated Troy's ass. I didn't think he had something like that in him. As low as Leon could be, I didn't think he would ever plot to kill me. Then again, for the right amount of money, who knew what Leon would've done? Hell, I never thought Leon would try to kill a man to be with the other man's wife. And not just any man, but his best damn friend.

Also, I was faking the hit plot because I kind of felt sorry for that dumb bitch Trice in a funny kind of way. But I quickly changed my mind. I said fuck it, let the bitch die, especially after I saw the pictures of that whore still visiting Leon

141

at the prison . . . that was it! Any little bit of sympathy for that home wrecker surely went right out the window when I realized those two were still up to their old tricks. That sneaky bitch was going to really die now. As soon as I knew about the visit, I brought Dray in on the deal to kill that stupid bitch.

The good thing was it didn't take much convincing to get Dray on board. He had a felonious past and no heart when it came to getting paper. I think Dray would probably knock off an old lady for his next buck. Just like me, he had grown up in the worst part of Norfolk, and he was always looking for that next dollar . . . no matter what it took. His story was the typical story for many young black men in the hoods of Norfolk—father missing, mother on crack, no education, and turned to the streets to survive or die.

Dray was a street nigga in every sense of the word. He smoked weed for breakfast, lunch, and dinner. He was a small-time hustler who never saved a fucking dime, because he spent all his money on weed, clothes, and bitches. But the most important thing was that Dray was ruthless and money hungry enough to kill a person . . . even a pregnant one.

At first, he was bugging off the fact that a man wanted to kill his pregnant wife, but after I told him the whole story, he was like, "Yo, let's get this bitch!" I had to laugh.

Dray had protected me since we were kids. But equally, he had done some fucked-up shit as well. In other words, we have had our ups and downs over the years. Once, Dray had done some foul shit to me when I heard that he had hooked Leon up with this chick name Angie. Dray said he didn't, but word on the street was Dray was just that foul. I had moved on, but I never really forgave Dray for that shit.

Bygones were bygones. I needed Dray. He was going to serve the purpose I needed—a real foolproof plan to get the money from Troy. Dray said he wouldn't actually get his hands dirty, though. I was kind of leery when he told me he knew somebody who could take Trice out for way less than the fifty thousand dollars I had told Troy to come up with. Dray convinced me the dude he had in mind could be trusted not to run his mouth in the streets or to the cops. That was all I needed to hear. Dray was gonna hit his boy off with like five g's; then he and I would split the rest of the money, and when Troy got that million-dollar insurance payout, I would just hit Dray off again with about half of my five hundred thousand. At least that was the way I presented the plan to Dray. I made him promise me that he would leave Virginia as soon as he got hit off, because niggas were jealous. We couldn't chance it.

The whole idea of having five hundred thousand dollars had Dray excited, and the best thing about that was Troy was none the wiser. That ass would just think I had Dray ready to do the hit all along. See, things always had a way of falling into place. And right now, things were falling into place for me perfectly. It wouldn't be long before I had enough money to get the fuck out of Virginia altogether and live in peace with my son.

Karma is a bitch—I tell you the truth.

I thought about how Leon ended up after doing me so dirty all these years. Then I looked at how Trice was going to end up after acting like she was wife extraordinaire all this time, when she was really just your typical lying-ass ho.

Everything just happened on chance when it came to this situation. I had stopped questioning it and chalked it up to fate. Finding out about Trice and Leon, getting those visit logs to show to Troy, and Troy getting insurance on his family the same day he found out his wife was a liar were all fate.

And I couldn't forget the most recent fateful turn of events. What if I hadn't been out in front of Troy and Trice's house looking for Troy's ass this morning? I would've never seen Trice leaving and decided to follow that bitch. Where did I follow her to? Right to the fucking prison, where, of course, that stupid bitch was visiting my fucking husband . . . again! Could anyone really be that fucking dumb or dick-whipped?

I had Dray jump out and take pictures of that

bitch. I wasn't going to let that one go unreported. I was definitely planning to show those pictures to Troy's ass. She had to be about the lowest, dirtiest bitch I'd ever seen. It was no wonder Troy was on the brink of knocking that bitch off. I guess he figured if he was going to get rid of a trifling ho, a payday might as well be involved. That worked for me. All I had to do was sit back and collect for the little bit of work I put in.

But first things first, this dummy needed to answer my calls.

"Call that nigga again. If he don't answer this time, I'm out. That nigga might be having cold feet or getting the cops involved. I ain't wit' going to jail, Charlene," Dray demanded. "I'm still on parole, remember?"

I picked up my phone and dialed Troy's number again. "Come on, fucker!" I growled. My heart almost melted when I heard the line stop ringing. Troy finally picked up his phone. I couldn't front, a warm feeling of relief washed over me. "Yo, nigga! You must be bugging the fuck out!" I screamed into the phone. Troy was quiet. "I told you that the dude wasn't one to be played with and you disappear for an entire day?"

"Look, Charlene, I'm not up for all of this drama. I needed a minute to sort things out. I told you that when I left the club," Troy said calmly. I looked at the phone like I wasn't hearing correctly.

"A minute to sort things out? What the fuck are you talking about? There is nothing to sort out!" I barked into the phone. "It's been a whole day! The hit has been planned and set up! This was all, you remember? There is no turning back now, Troy. I don't give a fuck what you gotta do—you better show up here with the fucking money or else these dudes are not going to be happy campers. I can't control what they will do to you from here on out. They want to get paid and that's the bottom line!"

Dray was standing close to me and listening. He had a hungry look in his eyes. I guess what I told Troy was the truth. Once I got Dray involved, there really was no turning back.

"I'm on my way there with the money," Troy said.

My heart jerked in my chest. For some reason, I expected him to make more excuses. But he really was going to come through.

"You got the whole fifty g's?" I asked, kind of stunned. Dray was smiling and punching his fist in the air excitedly. I put my finger up to my mouth to make sure Dray didn't make any noise.

"Yes, I got all of the money for the hit. Do you have proof for me that someone is really going to carry out the hit?" Troy asked. His question annoyed the shit out of me.

"You'll see when you get here. Meet me at the Marriott right now," I instructed. Troy blew out a long breath. "And, Troy . . . don't try no funny

146

shit, and just remember, there is no turning back. These niggas know what you look like and they know where you live," I warned.

"I hear you, Charlene. I'll see you in about twenty minutes," Troy said.

"Just in case you think this is not worth the trouble, I'm going to send you some pictures to your cell phone. Trust me, you'll want to see them," I said vindictively. Before Troy could utter another word or protest, I clicked off the phone and turned toward Dray. We both smiled like two Cheshire cats. We had to be thinking the same thing, because in all honesty this would probably be the easiest money either of us had made in our entire lives. I was overjoyed to say the least. No more shaking my ass, letting nasty niggas rub me up and down and treat me like a ho. Most importantly, no more sitting by taking shit off Leon. I was finally the bitch coming out on top! In my mind, there was no stopping me now.

"We did it! We're going to get paid!" I exclaimed, grabbing Dray by the shoulders. I started jumping up and down. I'm telling you, I could've just thrown a party right there. A few more hours and I would have thousands of dollars in my hands and it would all be mine!

"Yo, calm the fuck down, Charlene. You don't get excited until that motherfucking money is in your hands . . . ya dig? Plus, all that screaming and jumping up and down is blowing my high,"

Dray joked as he took a long toke off his blunt. "But we is about to get paid, though," he followed up, and the weed smoke escaped his mouth and made him cough. We both busted out laughing.

All my problems were about to be solved.

Or so I thought.

19

Troy

I was numb. I was completely emotionless and devoid of remorse about killing Trice after I saw those pictures of her at the prison. Again, she had gone behind my fucking back and went to see that nigga Leon. I just couldn't believe the level of betrayal my wife would stoop to. She was still going to see Leon. I couldn't believe this motherfucker used to be my best friend. And this bitch was still seeing this man. A man who almost took her life and mine!

Even though I didn't tell her I knew about her scandalous behavior with Leon, that bitch knew I had been different toward her since the last time she went and saw him and stayed away from the house all fucking day. Damn, I figured she would stay away from Leon and try to get our marriage back on track. That shit was just a pipe dream for me that I saw going up in smoke as I scrolled through Charlene's text pictures over and over again.

I was incensed. I never thought of Trice as a dumbass or a stupid bitch, but I was grossly wrong. This bitch had issues. *Did I really marry a stupid bitch and didn't realize it?*

All of that fucking being nice and sweet toward me was all a game to Trice. She played me like a fiddle over and over again. I admit, I was a nice, sensitive guy, but most women took that as weakness. I was about to show her ass just how strong I really was.

I felt like pure shit after my run-in with that bottle of Grey Goose and the cops. I had dragged myself around to pick up the cash I needed for Charlene . . . but it wasn't easy. The whole time I was locked up, I guess Trice had been leaving me messages and calling my phone. When I got my phone back, it was ringing as soon as I turned it on. Seeing that it was Trice made my blood pressure rise.

Lying bitch!

I continued to press IGNORE on my cell whenever she called. She'd left me a few messages, and as soon as I heard her voice, I pressed IGNORE. I didn't care what Trice had to say at that point. My mind wasn't even on the baby. I had long ago put that baby out of my fucking mind.

It had been a hard thing to do—facing the fact that I wasn't really going to be a father. I had had a lot of sad moments behind that shit. I'd even tried to drink myself into oblivion after realizing I had been so fucking stupid and had gotten played.

It's all going to be over now, though.

Even if I wanted to back out of this whole plan, I couldn't. Charlene was like a fucking thorn in my side. She was another one who kept blowing up my damn phone. I guess to a broke-ass bitch like Charlene, the prospect of all that money was like giving a starving man a cracker.

My plan was to meet with Charlene and give her the money, and then I planned to listen to Trice's messages one by one. I was thinking how wicked it would be to listen to her voice one last time before her ass was put out of her misery. I knew I'd feel better about the hit after hearing every single lying-ass message she left on my phone.

I mean, what would she say to explain where she'd been? "Oh, Troy, I was out shopping for the baby." Well, she couldn't say that shit, because I cut that bitch off from all of my money. "Oh, Troy, I was with my sister all day." She couldn't say that because Anna had already told me that Trice had not been hanging out with her. Anna said she was not going to cover for Trice, because she didn't agree with Trice cheating on me.

I shook my head as I thought about how Trice had made lying and scheming a way of life. It was something I had never expected from her. She had always been the consummate lady, always keeping it classy and taking the high road. Not after the spouse trade, though. She turned into nothing more than a hood rat in my eyes, and worse than Charlene could ever be. And that was saying a lot.

Charlene never fronted and acted like she was some classy chick. She was a straight-up hood rat from the word *go*. At least Leon knew what he was dealing with when it came to Charlene. She was up front and out there with her ghetto shit. She would tell you straight up that she was looking for where her next dollar was coming from. And her skank ass would do what it took to get it.

Not Trice. She was the dab-her-mouth-with-a-napkin type of dainty chick. She said prayer over her food before she ate, dressed conservatively, spoke proper English, without slang, and acted as if she were the perfect wife. She had people believing in those big hats and skirt sets she wore to church every Sunday. I knew better now. That bitch was no more than a wolf in sheep's clothing. I often wondered what she would have done to me if Leon were still out in the world. She probably would have taken me for half of everything, kicked me out of my own house, and had me paying her alimony while she shacked up with Leon. *Fucking bitch.*

I gripped my steering wheel until my knuckles turned white. My mind had painted the entire ugly and painful picture in my head of a happy Trice and Leon living it up on my dime. This whole visualization made me drive like a madman toward the Marriott. My chest was heaving up and down with a mixture of nerves, anger, resentment, and anxiety to get things over with.

I hadn't even thought through what I would do with my half of the million-dollar insurance money. I knew I would get the hell out of Virginia Beach. But I also knew I had to devise a plan to get Charlene and her thugs their share of the insurance money without them killing me. When I logically thought about this shit, the entire idea was fucking crazy. Like something out of a *Lifetime* movie.

But I was all in at this point.

Charlene had warned me there would be no turning back now, and I knew she meant business. Her wrath was something I wasn't up to dealing with. I was looking forward to the day I didn't have to hear her grating voice anymore. Although, I often thought one last blow job from Charlene would be great. She was the real *super head*. That bitch could suck an ear of corn out of a straw.

My tires finally squealed into the parking lot of the hotel and I parked. I let out a long, exasperated breath. This was the same place I had been nine months earlier, trying to get my wife and my life back.

The entire place unnerved me for a variety of reasons. I stared at the bag of money in the passenger seat next to me. Fifty thousand dollars was a lot of cash to let go of. But again, like Charlene had warned so many times, there was no fucking turning back now.

I stared at the Marriott's sand-colored building and wondered if I was really going to go through with this. My hands were suddenly trembling fiercely.

Then I picked up my phone and listened to some of Trice's messages. I needed to hear her lies. I needed confirmation that I was doing the right thing. I wanted motivation from her lying ass to take the money, pay the hit man, and move on with my life after she was dead. I pressed the phone to my ear so hard it stung.

The messages were all of Trice crying and asking me to meet her at home. She said she thought she was going into labor and needed me to be by her side. I couldn't front, my first instinct was to run to be at her side. I closed my eyes and felt something inside of me softening up. That's how I knew that deep down inside somewhere, I still loved my wife. *The bitch who would probably kill me herself if Leon was still free.*

After everything, I still hated to hear Trice upset. I hated to think of her in pain and helpless. I clicked off the phone. I had to catch myself real fast before I started my car back up and raced to be with my wife. Then I scrolled through and looked at the pictures again. The one of Trice's car stopped right next to the prison's sign. The one that confirmed that Trice had gone to see Leon again. The same photograph that convinced me she had serious issues. And as much as I wanted to laugh at her trying to hide her face on prison grounds, I really wanted to kill her trifling ass myself.

I was angry all over again. "You brought this shit on yourself," I grumbled as I balled my hands into fists. I told myself that Trice begging me to be by her side was so fucking foul, especially when she knew she had just betrayed me—again. What kind of fool did this woman think I was? Damn, she was really something else.

Hearing that shit burned me up inside. Was she really begging me to be a part of the birth of a baby she knew damn well wasn't fucking mine? I had to quickly pull it together. I knew I couldn't let Trice make it to the hospital to give birth before the hit happened, which meant I had to pay Charlene and her thugs, then stall Trice at the house so they could do their thing.

"Shit! This has to happen right fucking now!" I said. I grabbed the money off the seat, quickly exited my car, and raced into the Marriott lobby. I was sweating bullets and I couldn't remember the room number. "Fuck!" I cursed again. I needed to hurry up. I needed to focus. I was walking in circles in the lobby when the elevator doors dinged open. I had my head down as I rushed inside, and who do I run right into? The same state trooper I'd come face-to-face with on the side of the road not too long ago. I quickly averted my eyes away from him.

"You again?" Officer Cooley said.

"I'm just trying to check in here and get some rest. Clear my mind, you know," I said, my voice quivering with nerves. The officer looked at me kind of strange and then nodded.

"You better take care of yourself, boy. You ain't looking so hot," the officer said.

My phone vibrated in my hand. It was Charlene answering my text about which room to come to.

"I'm gonna do that, Officer," I said with a fake smile. I was glad when he stepped off the elevator.

I paced inside the elevator until it reached the sixth floor. I rushed out. I was a ball of nerves and felt as if my bowels would release right there in the hallway. I knocked on the door and Charlene pulled it back.

"What the fuck is wrong with you?" she asked after she gave me the once-over. "You look and smell like shit!"

I wanted to punch Charlene in the face. I wasn't in the mood for her stupid voice and her nasty mouth. I came here with one purpose, and it sure wasn't to be berated by her. I didn't even know how Leon lived with her annoying ass . . . good sex or not, she was a control freak. I was happy to be getting rid of her ass and soon!

"We have to hurry up! I think Trice is in labor and she wants to go to the hospital. We can't let that happen!" I whispered, rapidly pushing my way inside the room. I wanted Charlene's guy to take care of Trice and the baby all in one hit. There was no sense in having a baby that didn't belong to me on my hands. I wasn't about to care for that bastard's child. Charlene rolled her eyes at me. Of course, she was going to keep up this tough-girl charade.

"Charlene, we don't have time for your tough-girl display right now. This has to be done within a few minutes! I can only stall Trice at the house for a few more minutes," I gritted at her. Charlene's eyes widened like she was surprised to see me talking to her like that. I returned her gaze as if to say, *Yeah, let's stop the bull.*

"Dray! Dray!" Charlene called out. A tall, dark-skinned dude with stubby dreads came out of the bathroom. He was scary as hell and looked high as a kite. His presence in the room made me uneasy. I didn't like the looks of this character. I guess a hit man wasn't supposed to look like James Bond in a suit. I didn't really know what I expected from a chick like Charlene anyway.

"Why is you calling out my government, Charlene?" Dray asked, annoyed, as he eyed me evilly. I wasn't trying to hold eye contact with him. I immediately decided I didn't want shit to do with him.

"Don't yell at me!" Charlene snapped at him. "We only have a few minutes. Call the dude," she demanded.

I extended my hand with the bag containing the money, and she snatched the duffel bag. She tossed it to Dray and he opened it up. He smiled. It was an evil little grin. It gave me chills down my spine.

"Damn, nigga, you really gon' murk your wife for some bread?" Dray chuckled as he eye-screwed me. My nostrils flared at that statement, but I was too scared to say shit in return.

"Let's fucking go!" Charlene barked, extending a strange-looking cell phone. I noticed it was a throwaway phone.

"I have to call Trice and stall her at the house," I said nervously. They both looked at me like I was on crack. I put my hands up in front of me to calm them down. "I will tell her I'm on the way to meet her—that way she will still be there. Then I will call her when your guy is close and tell her that I changed my mind and I will meet her at the hospital. As soon as she leaves the house to get in the car, your guy has to be ready to pounce on her," I panted.

My heart was racing like crazy just thinking about what was going to happen soon. I felt kind of light-headed too. I didn't know if it was the hangover or if it was because I still couldn't believe I was going through with this.

"That's a good plan, Troy," Charlene told me. She turned toward Dray, her body animated. "Call that nigga right now!" she instructed him, flailing her arms.

I listened as Dray dialed his phone. "Yo, that thing is ready to go down. Yeah, here is the plan and the address," Dray stated.

I didn't know if I tuned him out or what, but I surely wasn't prepared for the chaos that erupted right after he started talking. It was as if I were having an out-of-body experience during what unfolded next.

20

Leon

The one thing I learned from all of the shit that went down with Charlene, Troy, and Trice was that karma was definitely a bitch when she reared her ugly head. I don't care who you are or what your claim to fame is—you can't outrun karma if you had all the money and resources in the world. Karma was even more fucked up when you were down on your luck like me. I guess losing both Charlene and Trice was the karma catching up with me for what I put Troy through. I just wondered what those two bitches were going to get in return for all the mayhem they had caused.

Even with the bad karma invading my space, I

still had a constant burning desire to have something happen to both of them. I often pictured Charlene and Trice dying slow, painful, horrible deaths with lots of suffering. Life was hard for me right now. I had to face the fact that I was behind bars and powerless. It was a hard pill to swallow. I was used to being the man in control of everything, including the bitches in my life. Not now. I had been reduced to nothing.

After my dustup in the visitors' room with Trice and then with those fucking COs who beat my ass afterward, I started carrying myself around the prison like I had nothing to live for. I was bumping niggas just for GP. I went in the day area and changed the TV channel just to dare a nigga to come after me. I was bullying niggas on their phone time, knowing damn well I ain't have nobody to call. It was like I just wanted to die. My own personal death wish. I was daring other inmates to come after me.

In truth, I didn't have shit to live for. All of my life, I had grown up thinking I was the man. My mother let me do whatever I wanted as a kid, but my sisters couldn't do shit. I walked around like I was the king of the castle. When I got older, it was the same shit. All kinds of bitches flocking to me validated my king mentality. Hell, they gave me anything I wanted. I was the shit!

When I met Charlene, she just made my head grow even bigger. In the beginning, she treated me like a king, and even after I did her dirty over and over again, she stayed with me and took my shit. Nobody could tell me I wasn't that nigga. Snagging a chick like Trice was the icing on the cake. She was what I grew up considering to be the "good, hard-to-get girl."

Those chicks were like putting together a puzzle or solving a mystery—a challenge. That's why dudes went after them so hard.

It hadn't taken much after all. When Trice decided to leave Troy for me, that made my head blow up to the size of King Kong's head. A nice, respectable, stuck-up bitch like Trice was willing to throw it all away for a nigga like me. I had to really think about that over and over. She was even willing to ride this bid with me. Nobody could tell me that my dick wasn't made of gold after that. I knew it wasn't my personality she was all crazy about. I mean, we had only spent that week together. Trice was throwing it all away for my dick. That was really what it boiled down to.

But all that shit had changed in an instant. Now I felt like a mouse trying to get a piece of cheese, instead of the man who once had it all. I wasn't the man at all. In reality, I was just another prison number with nobody checking on me. There were a lot of inmates like that in prison. They didn't have anyone bringing them money, visiting them, or even sending them socks and T-shirts. These dudes were in prison exchanging prison favors like washing niggas' drawers just to get a few cigarettes or commissary credit. I used to look down on them dudes. I used to say I was never going to be reduced to that shit. Now I was one step away from being just like them. The difference with me was I wasn't about to wash no nasty nigga's drawers for a cigarette.

I was lucky to still have some of the money Charlene and Trice had left on my books. I knew it would run out sooner or later, but in the meantime, I was saved from scrounging and doing prison favors to get by.

The COs came through the cellblock announcing it was chow time. That was always how I knew hours had passed. All of the hours seemed to be just one big blur since I didn't have anything to look forward to anymore. As soon as they returned me to my cell after my tirade, I had ripped up my calendar. I had only used the calendar to mark my Tuesday and Saturday visits.

I sighed loudly and got prepared to deal with another fucking meal behind bars. I was already thinking of what mischief I could get into to occupy the rest of my time for today. Nothing readily came to mind since I had done all the dumb shit I could think of. I climbed down off my bunk to head to chow. It was like any other chow hall, a lifeless waste of time. There was always day-old food that nobody wanted to eat.

Brother Mustafa had come back to the cellblock after his visit, and initially he looked at me like he felt sorry for me. Then he started lecturing me on Islam and its principles. At first, I wasn't interested. But soon, I started listening. I wasn't ready to convert and change my name, though. Brother Mustafa wasn't that fucking good at convincing me. I had become really cool with Brother Mustafa, and our initial fight was way behind us. I was in the chow line talking to him about how I planned to move on from the Trice situation when I heard someone behind me say, "Give me your tray, pussy." I ignored the voice. I didn't even turn around. I had no desire to see another chow hall fight. They happened so often that the COs just let the fights go down until they got tired of looking at them.

"I said give me your tray, nigga," the voice said again. This time, it seemed closer to me. I still didn't turn around. Niggas in the cellblock knew me, and they knew better than to be trying to son me over my food. Taking a dude's tray at chow was called making him your bitch in prison. That wasn't about to happen to me.

"Oh, you trying to act like you don't hear me," the voice growled, and then I felt metal connect with my skull.

"Oh, shit!" I exclaimed, dropping my tray and grabbing the back of my head. I knew then that the dude had been talking to me the whole time. I whirled around ready to pounce. There were about five dudes waiting. My eyes grew wide and my fists were ready. Before I could attack, they all rushed me at once. Pandemonium broke out in the chow hall. There were cheers and jeers erupting everywhere. I knew that I was doomed. The COs on duty weren't about to get involved until the ESU unit was called. Those were the dudes who came in riot gear with stun guns and shields. They took forever to come and save inmates too.

"This is for Charlene," one of my attackers growled. I was quickly thrown to the floor and pummeled. Punches, kicks, slaps, and any other form of violence rained down on my body. I couldn't tell from whom or even where the next punch or kick would come from. I tried to shield myself, because fighting back wasn't going to do it at that point.

I moved around, trying to dodge the punches, but that just made my attackers start kicking my legs. I even took a few shots to the balls. That was the worst pain I had ever felt. This had to be what death felt like. Pain ripped through my body like thunder, and I swore I could see lightning behind my eyelids. I threw my arms up, but I was being kicked and punched in the arms as well. It felt like a hard blow crushed the bone in my forearm.

My mind was fuzzy from the pain. I knew it wouldn't be long before I went into shock. My arm was hanging limp now. I tried throwing up my other arm. But before I could fully cover my face, a hard kick connected with my mouth. A sharp and intense pain ripped through my gums and teeth. "Aggh!" I managed to scream. I felt my front teeth spew from between my lips. I could feel and taste the blood filling up and dripping from my mouth. Blood also ran from my nose like a running faucet. My body throbbed all over, from my head to my feet. Another crushing blow to my chest took my breath away. It was taking an eternity for the COs to arrive and save me. With all of the folks Charlene knew, hell, the COs may be intentionally turning their backs to what was going on.

"You fucked with the wrong bitch! You did her dirty and now she is getting her revenge," one of the dudes growled as he punched me in the face. They were talking shit the whole time they were kicking my ass. Every now and then I managed to catch what was being said. I was too busy trying to stay alive to hear everything that was said.

Then my mind temporarily drifted to another thought: *I am getting my ass kicked.* Playing all bad since Trice dumped me, now I was getting what I deserved—*an old-fashioned beat-down.* And I didn't like it one bit. I'm sure my monkey-ass wife, Charlene, would've loved to see it.

Then out of a slight slit in my almost completely closed eyes, I saw someone come toward my chest with a shank. "Nah, my brother!" I heard Brother Mustafa's voice. "A fight is a fight, but I'm not going to let you stab this man while he's helpless."

"Mind your fucking business!" the attacker said. Next, there was more scuffling and kicks landing on my body.

"Oh, you want some of this too?" the dude with the shank asked Brother Mustafa. I knew then he had turned his weapon on Brother Mustafa. If I was spared being stabbed by the jagged piece of metal, then I owed my life to Mustafa. But I also knew if I didn't get shanked, someone had to. Being caught with a shank on your person was automatically another year or two on your time, and you could forget about probation forever.

I tried to scream out for a CO, but I was kicked in the face again. It felt as if shards of bone had shot directly up into my brain from that kick. With the beating I was taking, I couldn't even help Brother Mustafa. I could see him struggling. Then there was an influx of inmates with those beanies on their heads running our way— Mustafa's Muslim brothers. However, they were too late.

"Fuck you, Muslim-ass nigga," the dude with the shank said to Brother Mustafa. The next thing I heard was a low squealing. The noise came from Mustafa. I could see him holding his chest. Then there was so much blood. "Nooooo!" I tried to scream. My voice was weak, barely audible.

Brother Mustafa landed right next to me in a

heap. His eyes were open and a low hissing sound was coming out of his mouth. I hoped it wasn't his last breath. The Muslims began to counterattack the dudes who were beating me. But I knew they weren't there for me. They were there for a fallen brother, Mustafa. A man I initially disrespected when we became cellmates and the only one who came to my aid when I needed help.

Finally, the prison alarm sounded. That meant the COs were finally going to take care of the riot. It validated to me that my beat-down was approved by one or more of the corrections officers. If not, the alarm would have sounded when these dudes first started kicking my ass.

All of the dudes scattered and I finally heard the relieving sound of the COs from the ESU unit coming toward me. I was hurting real bad, but I still grabbed Brother Mustafa by his arm and tried to shake him to keep him alive.

"C'mon, man . . . don't die on me! You saved my life. Please don't die!" I rasped. Each word I said made the pain that racked my body even more pronounced. I could barely get enough air into my lungs to talk. I knew then that one of my lungs had been punctured by a broken rib.

I began drifting in and out, and black spots were manipulating my vision. Brother Mustafa let out one last breath before the COs quickly turned him over onto his back.

"Call the medical unit! Call them now!" one of the guards yelled to his counterparts.

I didn't know it then, but I would find out later that the worst thing in the world had happened because of these dumb-ass corrections officers. One of the Muslim brotherhood had died. Behind the walls, everyone knew that killing one of the Brothers was the worst act committed in prison. These were peaceful brothers who believed in unity amongst all races. By the COs failing to sound the alarm, one of the Brothers had lost his life—a life that would be revenged. I just hoped that I wouldn't be one of their targets.

There were screams and the sound of feet pounding on the floor. *Too little, too late.* I was being moved, but I couldn't feel my body anymore. It seemed like the pain was slowly fading away. I felt like I was drowning. I guess blood was filling up in my lungs.

I tried to cough, but then something happened. It was as if I were being snatched away. The next thing I knew I was hovering above my body and Brother Mustafa's. I could see both of us lying on the floor in pools of blood. It was as if I were on the ceiling and I could see all of the COs standing over us. They were looking around helplessly. They were no longer rushing or trying to help us. I was screaming at the top of my lungs, "HELP! HELP! HELP MY FRIEND!" But it all had to be in my mind, because no sound came out of my mouth as I watched myself lie still, surrounded by blood . . . my blood.

I kept screaming in my head. But no one could hear me. *The dead can't be heard.*

I'd heard people talk about how they could see themselves when something tragic happened to them. Now I was experiencing it firsthand.

I knew then that Brother Mustafa and I were both dead.

21

Trice

I could not keep still. I walked the floor inside the house, trying to keep my nerves and the pain at bay. I had already called my doctor and alerted him that as soon as my husband got home, we would be heading to the hospital. It was getting dark outside and the pains were coming fast and furious now. I had been calling Troy like a maniac for hours now. He was playing games, and I knew he saw that I had called him.

"Oh, God! Please, little girl, just give me a chance to get to the hospital," I groaned, speaking to my unborn daughter. I exhaled a long cleansing breath. The contraction was so bad I stopped moving and held my stomach. I heard my cell phone vibrating on the coffee table. I exhaled again.

"Hello?" I answered frantically. "Troy, where are you?" I huffed. He said something, but I wasn't even listening. "I think I'm in labor! I left you a bunch of messages! Now is not the time for you to have an attitude with me!" I screamed into the phone, panicked.

Troy was acting cocky after he had finally decided to call me back.

"Are you sure you'll be here in ten minutes?" I asked him after he told me to wait at home for him. "Please hurry up, Troy. I don't know how much longer I have. This is my first time having a baby, but I'm sure after all this time of being in pain that I have to be close to the end!" I wolfed.

Troy assured me he was on his way. I flopped down on the couch and used some of the breathing techniques I learned at the childbirth classes I had been taking. Even that method wasn't working anymore. I kept checking my watch, the cable box clock, the wall clocks, and my cell phone for the time. It was like an eternity, and Troy still didn't show up. Then after I had waited yet another hour, his dumb ass called back and said he couldn't make it home in time because he was stuck in traffic.

"Troy! Do you think this is a fucking game! This baby is coming any minute! I could've been gone already! Now you're telling me to drive alone, even closer to giving birth? What kind of man are you?" I barked in his ear.

Troy was quiet on the other end. Then he fucking calmly said, "Trice, there is no need to scream. Just drive yourself to the hospital and I will meet you there. Good luck."

What? Good luck? I had to actually look at the phone to make sure I was speaking to the right person. How could he be calm when his baby was about to come into the world? And just what the fuck did he mean, "good luck"? *What kind of man says that when he thinks his wife is in labor with his child?*

I could've jumped through the phone and kicked his ass. "You know what, Troy? Fuck you!" I screamed, and hung up the damn phone. I tossed my cell phone across the room in anger. I don't know how I managed to get off the couch, but when I finally did, I doubled over with another contraction. As bad as I felt, I knew I would need someone to help me so I walked over and picked my phone up from the floor. I thought about calling my sister, but I knew she'd make up some excuse about her kids or her latest man and I wasn't up for that. As bad as the pain was now, I was sure the baby was coming any minute. I had so much pressure in my vaginal area that I could hardly walk.

"You're so fucked up, Troy! You could've called me back hours ago and I would've been gone. I am in no condition to drive!" I screamed out loud as if Troy could hear me.

I doubled over for five minutes when another round of hard contractions ripped through my abdomen. I stood up straight again and caught my breath. "God, please let me make it to the hospital in time," I mumbled. I was so scared. I wobbled over to the table by the door and grabbed the two packed bags—one for me and one for the baby. I stood there for a few minutes until another hard contraction came and went. I touched my stomach for a few minutes and then I headed out the door.

I sat down in my car and prepared to pull out. "Shit! My cell phone," I cursed under my breath. I had forgotten to pick it up after throwing it across the room. I couldn't take a chance driving alone without a phone while I was in labor. If this baby decided to come, I would need to call 911 right away. I didn't know a damn thing about delivering a baby, regardless of how many birth shows I had watched.

I eased from behind the steering wheel again and stepped out of the car. I wobbled back into the house. Once I was inside, I heard the house phone ringing. I thought it was probably Troy, since I didn't have my cell phone. I picked up the cordless phone that sat near the door.

"Hello," I gasped into the receiver. I was expecting to hear a remorseful Troy begging me to wait for him. Boy, was I ever surprised.

"You should've never cheated on your husband, bitch! Especially with his best friend!" Wicked, cackling laughter followed. I looked at the screen, my face crumpling in confusion. The caller ID read *UNKNOWN*.

"Hello? Who is this?" I belted out. The call made me flush. I blew out a long breath as more pains hit me. I didn't have time to play phone games with some bitch. I got my cell phone off the floor, looked around one last time, and headed back out the door. I couldn't stop thinking about what the caller had said. Who would know about Leon and me?

I got into my car and began backing out of my driveway. Once I made it onto the street, I noticed a man on a motorcycle parked in front of my neighbor's house. He was just sitting there. I waved off any thoughts of how strange he looked as more pains hit me. I suddenly didn't give a damn about the strange man. I laid my foot on the gas and took off down the street. I barely wanted to stop at the stop sign on the corner of our street. I made a rolling stop and turned the corner. I drove a few feet and was stopped by a red light. That's when I noticed the dude on the motorcycle was following me. I squinted my eyes, peering into my rearview mirror at the dude.

"What the fuck is he doing?" I mumbled. I tapped on my steering wheel impatiently as I waited for the light to change. As soon as it did,

I stomped on the gas. My car zoomed down the street and so did the motorcycle.

"Shit! Is he really following me?" I asked out loud as if I were talking to someone else. "Oh, God, not more pains right now!" I cried out. This round of contractions made me pause. I couldn't even drive the pain was so bad. That gave the motorcycle time to catch up to me. I saw him ease up to my passenger window. I looked over and my eyes almost popped out of my head.

"Oh my God!" I screeched as I stared down the barrel of a handgun. "Nooooo!" I screamed, throwing myself down in the seat. The next thing I heard was the booming sounds of gunshots. *BANG! BANG! BANG!* Shot after shot rang out. My ears were ringing and I could feel heat engulfing my entire body. Glass shattered everywhere as the man kept shooting until he ran out of ammunition. My body was on fire everywhere, and I knew from experience that the feeling meant I was hit. Pain ripped through me worse than ever before.

"Help me!" I whispered. My throat was suddenly dry and my ears were clogged. The smell of smoke and gunpowder filled my nostrils. The smell was familiar and made me panic. I reached down with a trembling hand and touched my stomach. When I lifted my hand, I saw blood covering it.

"Help me!" I attempted to scream louder. My heart was racing and I could hardly breathe.

"Please!" I tried to scream again. "Save my baby," I cried.

Finally, I heard the motorcycle buzz away from my car. With my hands trembling fiercely, I reached under me for my cell phone in the cup holder. I pressed the button that automatically dialed 911. When the operator came on, I could barely get my words out.

"Nine-one-one, what's your emergency?" the operator droned perfunctorily.

"Please . . . someone shot me and I'm pregnant!" I rasped. "Pleeease!" I cried.

"Ma'am, who shot you? Where are you?" the 911 operator asked, seemingly coming alive.

"Please save my baby," I gasped. "Please."

"Help is on the way. Stay on the line so we can trace this call to your location. Please keep talking to me, ma'am," the operator said. Her words sounded like a record that was being slowed down. I could barely hear and my vision was becoming cloudy.

"Are you in a car, ma'am?" the operator asked.

"Yes," I answered weakly, barely able to talk. A very cold feeling was rising in my chest. I knew the baby wasn't moving anymore. I didn't know how I knew that when I was in so much pain, but I just knew.

"Do you know where you're shot?" the operator asked.

"My . . . my . . . sto-stomach . . . the . . . baby," I whispered, uttering each word laboriously. Speaking was taking too much of my energy. I could feel myself fading fast. I needed to tell the operator about the call I had received before I left the house.

"I think . . . someone purposely tried . . . to . . . kill me. I . . . I . . . think it . . . was . . . my . . . my . . . husband," I managed to get out. "Please, just save the baby's life . . . don't . . . don't . . . worry about me." Those were the last words I remember saying.

I heard the faint sound of sirens ringing from someplace distant. The walls were closing in on me. I felt overwhelmingly sleepy. I couldn't stay awake another minute. Everything around me went black. The last thing I remembered before losing consciousness was praying that the baby would make it.

22

Charlene

As soon as Troy passed me that bag filled with the money for the hit, I felt an overwhelming sense of power. It was like I had received a fucking sign from above. Dray was busy on the phone making the call to his boy who was going to carry out the hit, so that gave me time. I turned around real quick, dug into my purse, and gripped the 9-millimeter Glock I had hidden inside. I took a deep breath and turned on those motherfuckers like Judas. I knew Dray had taken his gun out while he was rolling his blunt. That nigga had gotten right comfortable since he thought his little cousin, Charlene, would never turn on his ass.

"Both of y'all motherfuckers put y'all hands up!" I gritted at them.

Dray and Troy both looked at me like I had lost my damn mind.

"Charlene, what the fuck is you doing?" Dray asked, his face folded into a frown.

"I'm holding y'all bitch asses at gunpoint until I get the fuck out of this room and don't think I won't shoot you," I replied, waving the gun in front of me.

"Charlene, I can't believe you're doing this shit," Troy had the fucking nerve to say.

"Oh, you can't? Well, I can't believe that you, Leon, and Trice did me dirty all these months! You wanted her, he wanted her, and me . . . little ol' me was left to the side. Well, not no more!" I barked at him.

"Well, I ain't do shit to you," Dray said, his hands still up in the air.

"You didn't do shit? Dray, you think I forgot all the times you stole shit from me when we was kids? You think I don't know you hooked Leon up with many bitches in the hood when I was your fucking cousin? Yeah, I know all about your grimy ass."

Troy and Dray were at a loss for words.

"Y'all are just like Leon . . . sleeping on little old hood rat Charlene. Nobody ever gave me credit for orchestrating something like this . . . fuck all y'all. Now, neither one of y'all better fucking move until I'm long gone. Troy, if you call the cops, I will tell them you put a hit out on your wife. Who, in my assessment, should be dead right about now. And you, Dray, I already got your PO on the way over here to bust you with the weed, so you better not try to fucking cooperate with no cops."

I grabbed my pocketbook and the duffel bag. The gun was still extended in front of me. "I'm not playing—do not try anything funny," I said as I backed toward the door. As soon as I put my hand on the doorknob, fucking Dray and Troy both tried to rush toward me. They must've thought I was playing!

BANG! BANG! I let off two shots. I heard shrieks and that was my fucking cue. I knew either one or both of them were hit. I was out the door in the next instant and rushing down the exit stairs. I didn't have time to wait for no fucking elevator. I knew hotel patrons would soon report the sound of gunshots. I threw the gun in my bag. I was fucking shaking, but I was not trying to turn back or get caught. I finally made it to the lobby door. Before I walked out of the stairwell, I took a deep breath and tried to act calm. I locked eyes with the front desk clerk.

"Excuse me, miss," the clerk said.

My eyes grew wide. "Yes?"

"Did you hear any fire crackers or gunshots?" the clerk asked me.

"Oh, no, I didn't." I smiled.

"Thanks," the clerk said; then he picked up the phone.

I knew his ass was calling the police. I finally hit the outside air. It was as if an unknown force were pushing my ass along. My legs were moving like I was Marion Jones running the 100-meter dash in the Olympics. My calves burned and my mouth was dry as the desert, but I knew I couldn't stop for shit. One wrong move and I would've been caught up. I had the duffel bag in tow, but I didn't let that shit slow me down one bit. I knew it was just a matter of time before someone at the hotel found Troy and Dray shot the fuck up in that hotel room.

I had to smile inside at how gangster I had been. I just snatched that bag of money, blasted my way out the door, and got the fuck out of there. I knew it would be a matter of seconds before the cops were swarming that Marriott again, just like when Leon had shot Trice. That was part of the reason I picked that spot.

I think I had hit Dray, because he kind of fell. But Troy I wasn't sure about. So far, everything was going according to the exact way I had mapped the shit out. All I had to do now was get my son and get the hell on. I had told my friend Delsey to meet me on the highway with my son. I was going to take that fifty g's, hit her off, and get the fuck out of Dodge with my baby. I never called off the hit on Trice either. As far as I was concerned, today was the day everybody got what was coming to them.

By now, if my calculations were right, Leon should have received the worst beat-down in his entire life, thanks to the three hundred dollars I left on the books of some dudes my friend hooked me up with inside the prison.

Troy got beat out of his money and for all I knew was dead from the shots I licked off on his ass.

Trice should be dead from the hit her husband put out on her.

Dray . . . well, let's just say he was a casualty of war. I couldn't trust him as far as I could see him. I knew Dray was a street dude, but anytime he got his hands on money, that nigga would go on a spending spree and bring mad attention to himself. I couldn't take a chance like that. The cops would have surely picked Dray's ass up after he got his hands on the money. I didn't know if he was snitch material, but I also wasn't trying to take a chance like that.

Bottom line, I did what I had to do for me and my son. I had learned early in life that nobody was going to look out for me but me. I was a changed woman. I intended to come out on top from now on.

My hands shook so badly that I could barely drive. As soon as I pulled onto the highway, I saw a line of police cars flying down the opposite side. I knew they were headed straight to the

Marriott. I shook off my nerves enough to part a small smile. I had gotten away with the loot and the revenge. I pulled into a Checkers parking lot and saw Delsey's car.

I exhaled and grabbed a stack of the cash. I raced out of my car and knocked on her car window. I saw my son's face and my heart just melted when he smiled and sang out, "Mommy! Mommy!" He was all I had in the world.

"Hi, baby! C'mon, we have to go fast. We are playing a new game, okay?" I said sweetly. Delsey looked at me expectantly. I quickly handed her a stack. She flipped through the bills and nodded at me with a wide smile on her face.

"Girl, I don't know what is going on, but you better get out of here," Delsey said, concern underlying her words.

"Please don't tell anyone about this, Delsey. I need to trust you. That is enough money to give you at least a three-week break from the club. Please, just do me that one last favor . . . keep your mouth shut," I pleaded.

She looked at me seriously and then she looked at my son. "I promise. You have my word, Charlene," she said sincerely. She gave me a quick hug and then pushed me away.

"Hurry your ass out of here with that beautiful boy," she urged.

I grabbed my son's hand and we rushed to the car. I strapped him into the backseat, and we peeled out of the parking lot. I let a long sigh of relief escape my lungs as I sped on the highway heading north. I was about to go start a new life someplace.

"I am *wife extraordinaire,* bitches," I said under my breath. I think somewhere in my mind the revenge was way more important to me than the money. The way all three of those motherfuckers had treated me had turned me into the monster that was driving away now, scot-fucking-free, while they all suffered. It was a great plan from the start and I must admit, those dummies helped me execute it perfectly!

"Hah!" I screamed out. Then I started laughing hysterically. I looked in the rearview mirror at my son, and he busted out laughing too.

We laughed and laughed.

23

Troy

I knew it! I fucking knew it! I was a stupid ass for ever trusting anyone in Virginia Beach or Norfolk!

I felt like kicking my own ass for letting my guard down. Everything happened so fast that I couldn't even react. It was surreal, like I was living a nightmare. I should have known not to trust a bitch like Charlene. I had learned real quickly that I had made a grave mistake. One minute, everything seemed to be going as planned. I was at the Marriott, handing over more than half of my retirement fund to Charlene for the hit. I was confident I was going to collect it back and then some later after Trice's death. Hell, now I didn't know what was up. I didn't know the status of

Charlene's hit man. I know Dray called in the hit to his contact, but that was the size of it.

I was thinking, *This is all perfect.* It was exactly how things were supposed to go. Initially, I felt a great sense of relief, and admittedly, I was kind of excited that it would all be over very soon. But that feeling was snatched away so quickly I didn't know what hit me. I had my hands shoved down into my pockets listening to Dray give his hit man the order. I had provided Trice's car make and model and my home address and he was relaying it just as I had provided. I was listening to him so intently as he drafted the plan to kill Trice that I wasn't even paying Charlene any attention.

Dray finished his call and turned around to tell Charlene everything was set. But neither one of us was prepared for what we heard next. Charlene was barking something from behind us. When I turned around, that crazy-ass bitch was pointing a gun at me and Dray. My eyebrows dipped so low, they almost touched the bridge of my nose. I was shocked and confused to say the fucking least.

"What the fuck——" I began to say, but Charlene's crazy ass cut my words short. She was waving the gun in front of her like a madwoman.

"Yo! Whatcha——" Dray started too.

We looked at each other, then looked back at Charlene.

"Don't say a fucking word. Neither one of

y'all. I will shoot both of you bastards if y'all don't let me get out of this fucking room with this bag of money," Charlene growled. Her voice wasn't quivering with nerves or anything. She had her lips pursed and she spoke through clenched teeth. Her eyes seemed to be flashing with fire. Her face was stony and cold, like a woman scorned times one million.

Charlene gave the rundown on how everybody had done her so dirty and that this was all her plan to get revenge. Her words hit me like a ton of bricks. She was right. During the spouse trade, I had shunned her like she was a diseased dog. Leon had cheated on her with Trice, and after Charlene went back home, she had busted him making plans to leave her for Trice. Trice was the prized possession, so all of the attention was on her, which made Charlene seem like the bottom-of-the-barrel bitch. She had caused a lot of mayhem during that whole time, but I never thought she had done all of that because she was hurt deep down inside.

"Charlene . . . we can talk about this," I said, putting my hands up in front of me in surrender.

"No! Ain't shit to talk about!" Charlene screamed, continuing to wave the gun.

That's when shit just suddenly went downhill fast. I think Dray lunged toward her, but I couldn't be sure because things were unfolding so fast I couldn't keep track. I knew my heart was pounding so fast I could feel it in the back of my throat. I was sweating—I was sure of that. I could feel beads of sweat sliding down my back.

Then it happened. That crazy bitch lifted that fucking gun, trained it on me and Dray, and pulled the trigger. "Nooo!" I screamed, but it was to no avail. I felt the hot metal pierce my skin somewhere, but I couldn't be sure where. "Oh shit!" I said before stumbling backward and then falling.

"You crazy bitch!" Dray hollered. It was too late. Charlene had moved like a fucking gazelle running from a hungry lion. She was out of that room in a cloud of gun smoke.

I couldn't believe that shit. Even if she had threatened us with the gun, I never expected her to actually shoot us. I was on the floor and pain gripped me. I was scared to move at first, but I had to know where that searing pain was coming from. I moved a trembling hand and felt around on my body. Finally, I felt my shirt and the left side was soaking wet.

"Aggh!" I moaned, gripping my side. I was shaking like a leaf on a tree in a wild storm. I had never experienced that kind of pain in my entire life. I moved my hand across my side and under my shirt. It was wet and there was definitely a hole in my skin. The entry wound in my side still had heat rising out of it from the hot bullet.

"Oh, shit. Man . . . I'm hit. I'm hit bad," I moaned to Dray. I lifted my hand to my face and saw dark maroon blood covering the entire palm of my hand. The smell was so pungent and strong, like newly cut raw meat with a tinge of metal. I believed the very dark color of the blood could be a sign that the blood was coming from an organ and not just a little flesh wound.

"Aggh! I can't believe that bitch shot me!" I managed to scream through the puffs of air I was letting out from the panic that had taken over me. Trying to talk and even to breathe just made the pain worse. It felt as if a flamethrower had blown fire into my chest and lower abdomen. I couldn't tell where exactly Dray was because it was like he had just disappeared. Suddenly, he came rushing out of the bathroom.

Great, *now* he had his gun. Some good that would do us now! I kept my eyes on Dray. He didn't seem to be shot. His ass was frantic, though. He was stalking around like a damn madman, as if he was looking for something.

"Help me," I said to Dray, my voice strained. It took a lot to muster up enough to speak.

"Yo! I don't know what to tell you about that problem you got there. You can't go to no hospital. Gunshot wounds are mandatory for doctors to report. Those fucking cops will be there in a few minutes flat if you go to the emergency room and shit," Dray rambled.

I couldn't believe the selfish shit he was saying. "Please," I whispered.

Dray was shaking his head. "Nah, I can't afford to be no witness in no shooting," Dray said in a panicked tone. "My fucking parole officer will violate me on the spot. I can't have that. Nah." He was sweating as if he'd just run a marathon. I, too, was sweating because I was in pain and my body was burning up from the gunshot. I think Dray had a serious case of panic setting in.

"I will die if I don't get some help," I groaned, pressing on my wound harder in an attempt to suppress the bleeding. Dray was walking around in circles like he didn't know what to do next, while I lay there with what could be only a few minutes to live.

"This bitch Charlene is going to pay. She fucked with the wrong nigga now. Family or no family . . . that bitch is going to die!" Dray gritted.

Finally, he stopped pacing and picked up his cell phone. After he dialed a number, he started pacing the floor once again. He was making me dizzy just watching his ass. He didn't even have the decency to help me up onto the bed from the floor.

Dray dialed a few numbers before he finally made a connection to whomever he was trying to reach. "Yeah, nigga! It's me, Dray. You ain't gon' believe this shit. My cousin, Charlene. Yeah, that bitch took the money. Nah, I'm dead-ass serious. She fucking left here guns blazing, shot at me and shot this fucking lame-ass nigga and left! This nigga laying here dying."

What the fuck? I'm lying here dying and this mother-fucker is calling me a lame-ass nigga? "That's right . . . I want her found and brought to me!" Dray barked into the phone. He finally said he wanted her dead. For someone who didn't want attention brought to the room, he was surely talking loud. That's how ignorant his ass was. I was rocking my head back and forth on the floor, trying to keep from losing consciousness. I had seen enough cops and drama shows to know that if I lost consciousness, it sped up the dying process.

I was frustrated but helpless to save myself. I was too scared to try standing up. I didn't think I had enough energy to even make it up onto my legs. "Dray. Please help me," I begged. He just glared at me.

I don't think Dray understood how important it was for me to get some medical help. He seemed as if he was contemplating it. I was silently praying that he would have a change of heart at any minute.

All hope was lost when there was a knock on the hotel room door. I stopped moving my head. At first, I thought I was hearing things. There were more knocks. Dray jumped at first; then he froze in place. With his eyes stretched to their limits, he looked at the door. Next, he looked down at me. He folded his face into a tough-guy expression and rushed over to where I lay. Then he got down on the floor next to me, which took me aback. He was facing me and got close to my face. So close I could feel and smell his hot and stale breath on my face.

"Shut the fuck up and don't open your mouth. We are not answering that fucking door," Dray whispered harshly. My eyes were starting to flutter, but I saw that he had his handgun gripped tightly in his hand. He wasted no time making his point when he pointed his gun right at my head. I don't know why I didn't just scream anyway. I guess if you've been shot once and know what it feels like, you'd be silent too.

"You better not fucking say one word until I can get myself out of this fucking room," Dray growled.

I nodded. Tears escaped the sides of my eyes and pooled in my ears. It was a combination of helplessness, regret, and overwhelming pain that caused me to cry at a time like this. It was like a nightmare I just couldn't wake up from. Not only was my wife probably lying dead somewhere thanks to me, but also I probably won't even be alive to collect one dime of insurance money. Meanwhile, Charlene was free and clear.

"Ugh," I grunted as a wave of pain shot through my chest. I knew my heart was preparing to give out. It was becoming harder for me to breathe now. My lungs were probably filling up with blood too. Dray was tiptoeing around the room. After the second round of knocks at the door, this idiot tiptoed over and peeked through the curtains of the hotel room window.

He turned back around like he'd seen an army of ghosts.

"This shit is serious, man. The police are crawling all over the fucking place out there. What the fuck I'ma do now?" Dray said, his voice quivering. "I can't afford to go back to the joint." His facial expression told me he was scared as shit. Not such a tough street dude anymore.

I had to think quickly, because Dray obviously was in no state of mind to think of a plan to get us out of there. I already knew niggas like Dray weren't the sharpest tacks in the box. So I figured I'd try some psychology on him, anything to get him to seek medical help for me.

"You didn't shoot me, so they won't arrest you. We can say we were robbed or something. It's not totally a lie, right?" I gasped, wincing with each word. "You can say you're my brother and some strange guys pushed inside and robbed us," I continued through the pain. My voice was getting weaker and weaker. I started feeling a funny buzzing in my head too. I knew it wasn't going to be much longer before I passed out.

"Please . . . Dray . . . I'm bleeding real bad, man," I pleaded. "You rather be in here with a gunshot victim and say we got robbed . . . agghh . . . rather than end up in this hotel room with a dead body and no witness to help you explain the story," I managed to say. By the time I got all of those words out, my mouth was desert dry and my tongue felt lead heavy.

194

"Shit! Shit! Fuck!" Dray cursed. He must've thought about what I was saying. I would be dead and then how would he explain that, especially since we were on the sixth floor with only one way out of that fucking room—the door.

I closed my eyes and said another silent prayer that this dumb nigga would come to his senses and try to get me some help. My eyes shot back open when more knocks erupted on the door.

"Police! We need to speak to all hotel patrons!" a voice filtered in from behind the door.

Dray came completely undone when he heard the police speaking through the door. He started moving around real fast. He was sweating and in a panic. He was waving that fucking gun around, which scared the shit out of me.

"Calm down, Dray," I gasped. I didn't know what else to say. He looked totally crazed. Then more knocks came, so Dray stopped moving. His chest was heaving up and down rapidly.

"Yo . . . I can't go back to the joint. They will kill me if I ever come back. I ratted on them niggas, man," Dray said, whining like a straight-up bitch. He was about to break down crying. Although I was in crazy pain, I just couldn't believe this shit. He was going to let me lie there and die because he was a snitch who was scared to go back to prison. In other words, a pussy! How did he even know they would send him to the same fucking prison? What a selfish prick!

"Please, Dray," I rasped again. It was one last-ditch effort to make him come to his senses. I thought about yelling out to the cops on the other side of the door, but I quickly dismissed that idea. Shit, I couldn't take the chance because Dray still had the gun and he was clearly unstable.

"They gonna know something as soon as they come up in here, man. They gonna blame me for shooting you. They gonna arrest me. They gonna violate me. I can't go back to the joint . . . I'm telling you . . . I just can't," Dray whined some more. Whomever he snitched on must be very powerful, because I'm telling you this dude was on the verge of tears. I was also on the verge of tears, because I didn't know what he would do next.

"Open up or we're coming inside. We can hear you in there," the police called out.

A flash of fear welled up inside of me. Those fucking cops just didn't know how much damage they were doing by banging on the fucking door. I was silently praying that the cops would just be quiet and get the balls to bust the fucking door down and rush inside.

"Shit, man," Dray cried, moving his arms wildly. I knew he was going to put me out of my misery.

"Dray, man, we . . . we can get out of this," I stammered. The words were labored. That was it—I couldn't say another word. I had absolutely no energy left in my body. I decided that this was how things would end for me, dead on the floor of the Marriott after putting a hit out on my own wife. It was karma at its best.

I lay there staring blankly, waiting for the grim reaper to come get me. Then, in the blink of an eye, Dray lifted the gun to his head and before I could scream out, he pulled the fucking trigger. *BANG!* One shot to the temple took him out within seconds. His blood splattered all over my face.

It all seemed to unfold in slow motion. I could feel my mouth open wide, but I couldn't muster enough energy to scream. I felt vomit creeping up my esophagus. My heart was going crazy and blood seemed to spew faster from my wound. Dray's body fell so close to me, his dead, glassy eyes were staring directly into my eyes.

"Help!" I finally rasped. I didn't have to call out for long. After the sound of the gunshot, the police busted into the room with their guns drawn. They pounded into the room like a swarm of angry bees.

"Police!" I heard them yelling at first. "Oh, shit!" one of them said.

"Get two buses here now!" one of the cops yelled. *Bus* was cop talk for *ambulance.*

It was pure chaos. "Two black males, one deceased, one still alive but shot!" More yells. I finally let myself go.

Either they would get me help or I would be dead . . . just like Dray.

24

Trice

My eyes popped open and I suddenly couldn't breathe. I awakened in a panic. My baby was the first thing that popped into my mind. *Where is she?* I wanted to hold her. I couldn't move my head. It felt as if I was being restrained by something. My arms came alive next, and instinctively, I grabbed for the plastic tube that was shoved deep down my throat. I could feel myself gagging against the annoying contraption. It was held in place with tape that contorted my mouth. I tried to scream, but the breathing tube kept any sound from being released.

My eyes darted from the ceiling and then they went wild, scanning my surroundings. I could see blurry silhouettes at the end of my bed. There were at least four of them huddled together. They were moving, engaged in some kind of meeting it seemed. Possibly having a discussion. I could tell they were talking, because I heard low mumbles rising from the area where they were standing.

I had no idea where I was or how long I had been there. That thought alone brought another wave of panic to my chest. I weakly yanked on the breathing tube as hard as I could. But I had no strength in my arms. Weakness controlled my whole body.

Suddenly, I heard alarms ringing over my head, to the left and right of me. Then the silhouettes came into focus. They had on white coats and were holding clipboards. They dispersed from their meeting and moved closer to me. All of their faces registered shock and horror as I continued to flail and yank at tubes.

"She's awake. She's trying to remove the breathing tube." I could see and hear a petite female Indian woman in a white coat. I surmised she was a doctor. There were a lot of loud murmurs, pointing, and two of the white coats ran out of the room calling for a nurse.

"Bring a sedative right away!" a tall black doctor instructed. His face was serious, grave looking, even as he took in an eyeful of me. He rushed to my side and grabbed my hands. "Okay, okay," he said. He splayed his body over mine and used it as a human restraint.

"Mrs. Davis . . . we need you to calm down. I know it is strange waking up in a hospital bed full of tubes, but it was necessary to save your life. Please, just calm down," the black doctor said, his voice soothing.

I was moving my mouth, but no sound came out. A rough, grating noise escaped my mouth instead.

"Shhh, don't try to talk," the doctor continued. "You have to wait until we evaluate your lung to see if you can breathe on your own before we consider removing the tubes."

I finally stopped flailing and kicking. His body seemed to relax against mine. His eyes flashed concern and pity for me. I closed my eyes, exasperated. I wanted to talk. I had so many questions. I couldn't remember anything, including how I got there. At that moment, I didn't remember much. My body was weak, my mind frail. I could only think of one thing: *I wanted to see my baby.*

After I was still for a few minutes, or maybe it was a few seconds, I really didn't know, the doctor looked at me seriously. "Are you calm now? Can I get up?" he asked in a sweet baritone voice. I nodded in acquiescence. "Don't make me regret letting you go free," he replied, raising one eyebrow.

As he lifted himself up, the nurse appeared behind him with a syringe. She headed for my IV bag. "This is just something to make you relax," the nurse said as she glared at me as if I were a bad child being reprimanded.

"Wait," the doctor said, halting her actions. The nurse stopped and looked at him like he had lost his mind.

"But, Dr. Jackson . . . the patient is hysterical," the nurse stated, her tone sassy and demanding. She was clearly annoyed with him.

"I know, but she's calmed down now. Let me at least talk to her for a couple of minutes before we put her back out. We both know why she awoke in a frenzy," Dr. Jackson said.

"Whatever you say. You're the boss. But if she—"

Dr. Jackson cut the nurse off abruptly. "If she does anything to harm herself, I will take responsibility. And you're right, I am the boss, so please," Dr. Jackson snapped. The nurse looked like she had swallowed her words. She scurried away like a wounded puppy.

Dr. Jackson turned his attention back to me. He cracked a small, halfhearted smile. He patted my leg softly. "Now, you behave and don't get me in trouble," he said.

I closed my eyes to let him know I would behave. I lifted my hand and touched my stomach. I questioned him with my eyes.

The doctor let out a very long sigh. "Mrs. Davis, you definitely suffered some very grave injuries. We had to work really hard to keep you alive. You lost a lot of blood, and when you lose blood like that while you're . . ." Dr. Jackson rambled.

I became impatient. He was playing games. No, he was beating around the bush. I could tell he was stalling. He knew exactly what I was asking him about. I started banging my hand on the bed. The heart monitor began beeping like crazy. I banged and then I touched my stomach. My chest was heaving.

"Okay . . . okay . . . Mrs. Davis, just please calm down. You can't afford to hyperventilate when you can't breathe on your own. I will tell you about the baby," Dr. Jackson replied.

I felt the heat of relief wash over me. I was glad he knew what in the hell I was talking about. I stared at him intently, telling him with the burn of my gaze to get to the fucking point. He let out a long sigh.

"Mrs. Davis, as I was saying before. When you're pregnant, blood flow is what feeds your placenta, which is what feeds your baby. When you were shot, you lost so much blood that the placenta could not continue blood flow to the baby . . . ," the doctor said. His eyes looked glassy. I held his gaze. My heart rate sped up. I could feel it and I could also hear it on the monitor. Fear gripped me around the throat like a choke hold.

"Mrs. Davis . . . your baby daughter, unfortunately, didn't make it. She didn't stand a chance in the womb with that amount of blood loss, and bullet fragments also hit her. In fact, from the angle that the gunshots hit your car and your body, if it wasn't for the baby being inside of you blocking some of your vital organs . . . you would have died yourself. We have pictures of the baby for you," he said, reaching into his pocket.

He retrieved two Polaroid-style pictures and held them in front of my face. I stared at the image of my daughter. She looked exactly like Troy. Tears formed in my eyes and ran down my face.

"Mrs. Davis, I am really sorry. She is in the morgue being held for a proper burial when you are better," Dr. Jackson finished.

His words exploded in my ears like small bombs were being dropped around me. My baby daughter was dead. And she really was Troy's baby. I couldn't explain the feeling that came over me.

I wanted to die.

This time, he didn't even have time to react. I yanked that fucking breathing tube straight out of my mouth. A hissing sound filled the room as the air from the tube escaped. I still couldn't muster enough breath to scream. I was flailing, kicking, and moving my head in wild circles. I yanked the IV from my arm and blood shot across the room.

Dr. Jackson began moving. He called for the nurse again. "Bring the sedative! Bring the sedative now!" he hollered.

The nurse walked slowly, rolling her eyes and taking her time. "An *I told you so* is in order here, Doctor," she said.

"Now is not the time to point fingers!" Dr. Jackson retorted.

I was going crazy on the bed. I wasn't trying to let them stick me with the syringe filled with sedatives. I didn't care if I died; I wasn't letting them give me the breathing tube or IV. I didn't want any heart monitors. I didn't want anything that would help keep me alive. I wanted to die. I fought a good fight and in my weakened state, that wasn't much. But it did take two doctors and two nurses to finally restrain me enough to stick me with the needle.

I felt the sedatives taking over me, but I kept trying to fight against them. Each time my eyes dipped low, I would fight to keep them open. I wanted to kill myself. I wanted those fucking doctors and nurses to let me die. I wanted to be with my baby in heaven.

Just as I was about to finally conk out from the losing battle I was fighting against the meds, I caught the cloudy silhouette of two men walking into my room. From what I could still make out, one was short, the other tall. One was black and the other was white.

They were staring down at me. No, more than that. They were trying to converse with me, and from what it looked like, I think they actually expected me to respond. But the drug was working. I didn't hear what they said and I definitely couldn't respond.

The last thing I saw were their matching beige trench coats. And I was sure I heard the words *homicide detectives.*

Finally, the sedatives defeated me.

And I was defeated.

I couldn't see or hear anything else except the image of my dead daughter on the inside of my eyelids.

25

Charlene

After hours of driving, I finally decided to stop when I made it to Delaware. It was the halfway point between Norfolk and New York City, which was where we were headed. Yes, the big city was where this little country girl was going to make a new life. I had been there once or twice to shop, and I loved the hustle and bustle of city life. No little town for people to be all up in your business like in Norfolk. Besides, I had been feeling like it was time for me to leave Virginia for a long time. I just never had the resources to do it before now.

I figured in New York, I could blend in with the huge city crowds and just start over brand-spanking-new. I was sure it would take some getting used to, but I was ready. I was so fucking ready it wasn't even funny anymore. I had been done dirty one too many times. Leon, Troy, and Trice didn't think I would land on my fucking feet after everything that happened. I guess I showed them.

I planned to take Troy's hit money and put it to very good use. I knew I had that money free and clear, no strings attached. It was all mine.

Every now and then, as I drove, I thought about how to make that money last. I figured I might go into business or something. I always wanted to own a hair salon. That was something I was seriously considering. I had always wanted to be in the beauty industry, but years of being verbally berated by Leon had discouraged me from pursuing anything that would better myself.

I had also spent too much time worrying about how many bitches he was fucking to think about furthering my education or getting my cosmetology license. I mean, my marriage to Leon had definitely taken a real toll on me. I had given up so much to be with him and in the end what was it all for? Nothing! Look where that had gotten me.

The thoughts of the past, present, and future were crowding my head. I was obsessing too hard about what to do next. I was giving myself a headache, plus I was exhausted from the events that had taken place back in Virginia. I knew that whatever I decided to do with my life from this day forward, I had to work like a motherfucker to make this fifty thousand dollars work for me. That wasn't a whole lot of money, and it damn sure wasn't going to last forever. Making it grow into something my son and I could live off of was my main goal. I thought the concrete jungle—New York City, where dreams were made—was the place I could make that happen.

If my thinking was right, I knew by now that fucking Dray probably had all of the goons he could find in Norfolk looking for my black ass. Dray was probably cursing my name and thinking I was the grimiest bitch alive. I had definitely used his ass to get what I wanted. Oh well, he wasn't thinking about me when he was stabbing me in the fucking back either.

I wasn't sure about Troy trying to find me or report what I did to him. I mean, what was he going to tell the cops? He damn sure couldn't tell them I robbed him of the money he was going to use to pay for a hit man to kill his wife. He was probably smart enough to know that I had recorded some of our phone conversations, so I'd have proof if he ever did go to the cops and report me. On that end, I wasn't worried about Troy at all.

This money was mine and that was the bottom line. Dray would probably never go to the cops either. That nigga was so scared of going back to the joint that if he even saw cops, he would walk ten blocks out of his way to avoid them. I had planned and timed my whole shit just right. I smiled every time I thought about how smoothly that shit had gone down. I didn't think I would have the balls to shoot at them, but when it came to being either them or me, I started licking off shots like I was a motherfucking marksman.

I was that bitch for real.

I gripped the steering wheel and shook my head. I kept yawning. "Okay, Charlene, it might be time to stop. You can't drive the hell off the road," I mumbled to myself.

I checked the rearview mirror and looked at my son in the backseat. He had finally fallen asleep after whining and crying about wanting to get out of the car. I knew it was definitely time to stop when my vision started getting blurry. I was tired as hell, my emotions were riding high, and my son was clearly uncomfortable being in the car for so long. He was too young to understand how important it was for us to get as far away from Norfolk as possible. He had asked for his daddy more than once too. I would just change the subject and start singing songs with him. I still hadn't decided what I was going to tell him about Leon. Plus, I still wasn't sure if Leon had even received the beat-down I had so evilly sent to his trifling, cheating, dirty-dog ass.

I pulled into a Residence Inn near the Christiana Mall. I looked in the visor mirror and fixed my wig. I also put on the hazel contacts I had purchased during the planning phase of my little plan. I couldn't be too careful. For all I knew, cops could be looking for me on a national manhunt.

I peeled off a few dollars from the money in the duffel bag. I didn't want to open it in public. I also took Delsey's driver's license out and looked at it one last time. She didn't know I had stolen that shit out of her bag one night at the club. I had even helped her look for the shit the next day when she complained about losing it. Oh well. I had to do what I had to do. People always said she and I could go for sisters. With the wig on, I did kind of resemble her picture.

"Come on, baby," I said, shaking my son awake. He groaned a little and rubbed his little eyes. I put the duffel on my shoulder and grabbed his little hand. "We're going on vacation, okay?" I said to him. He just groaned again.

"We gonna play a little game. My name is going to be Delsey, and your name is going to be Russell, okay?" I told him. He nodded his agreement. "So, if someone inside the hotel asks you what is your name, what will you say?" I asked for clarification.

"Leon Junior," my son said. A flash of panic flitted through my chest. I bent down and got eye level with him.

"No, baby . . . remember . . . you have a new name now. Your name is Russell Parker. My name is not Charlene . . . it's Delsey, like my friend. We have to make pretend these are our names or monsters are going to come get us. Understand?" I said, looking my son in the eye and speaking in a serious tone. He looked like he was kind of scared. I didn't want to be so fucked up as to scare my baby, but if it was going to be the only way I could get him to go along with the new identities, then so be it.

"Okay, Mommy. I don't want the monsters to get me, so my name is Russell and your name is Delsey," my son repeated.

I lightened my mood and smiled at him. "Come here, big boy. You are so good that to-morrow Mama is going to take you and buy you a treat," I told him as I gave him a strong squeeze.

"Yay! What kind of treat? Where we gonna go?" He was excited. He started asking me a million questions as we walked into the hotel lobby. I was happy that he was distracted when I stepped up to the front desk. I was so nervous that I was stammering like an idiot when I asked for a room. The clerk raised an eyebrow when I asked to pay for the room in cash.

"Well, ma'am, we usually still ask for a credit card to put on hold," she said.

My heart started beating fast and I felt hot all over. I had to think fast. "I left my bag with all of my cards in it. I have cash—" I tried to explain.

"I'm gonna have to ask my manager," the girl interrupted me.

I gave her a pleading look. "Listen, I am running from an abusive husband. I can't afford for him to find me and my son because he'll try to kill us. Please . . . will you just help me," I whispered with fake tears rimming my eyes. The girl looked at me with sympathy. She clasped her hand over her mouth.

"Please," I whispered, sliding a hundred-dollar bill in her direction. The girl's eyes popped open and she looked around to make sure no one else could see her accepting the cash. She slid it off the counter and slipped it into her pocket. She lowered her eyes and started pecking on her computer. A warm feeling of relief washed over me and I let out a long, exasperated sigh.

"You will be in room 615, ma'am. Continental breakfast is served every morning from six to ten," the girl said, her words coming out in rapid succession. I could tell she wanted to get rid of my ass, and I sure wanted to get the hell out of that lobby.

"Is there Internet?" I asked.

"Oh, yes, ma'am, free Wi-Fi access . . . Here is the code," she said as she slid me my room keys. I winked at her and then I mouthed the words *thank you* silently. I grabbed Leon Jr. and we headed toward our room.

I was so intent on getting a hot shower and a warm bed that I never noticed anyone watching me, much less following me.

In fact, I thought I had been extra careful when I drove out of Virginia, but I guess one can never be that careful.

26

Troy

I wished I were unconscious when the police kicked in the door at the Marriott. I wanted to forget all the shit that had occurred. From Charlene robbing and shooting me to Dray dying by his own hand—and I didn't want to think about Trice. My mind was all over the place. But even so, it kept coming back to the pain I was in.

I was shot in the side somewhere. I was sure I had been bleeding for at least twenty to thirty minutes, and I figured if I blacked out, it would be much easier to deal with and handle all of the recent events. I didn't want the cops asking me a whole bunch of probing-ass questions about what had happened. Not with my fucking lousy luck. I had my eyes closed, but them shits were flickering like a motherfucker. With all of the chaos going on around me, I couldn't fake unconsciousness even if I were an Academy Award–winning actor.

"We need paramedics!" I heard cops calling over their radios.

"We are getting you some help," one cop said as he kneeled down over me and put two fingers on my neck to check my pulse rate. "Can you hear me?" he asked in my face. I just kept my eyes closed. "He is not unconscious, but I guess he can't speak," the cop said to some of the others who were now pillaging the hotel room for evidence. With everyone talking and shouting at the same time, it was hard picking up every conversation or word spoken.

But that was a great fucking story the cop had just given me. If I lived through this, I knew that detectives were going to ask me mad questions. These uniformed cops had just given me a great idea of what to say. I felt a little better about the situation. Initially, I was scared as shit. There was no fucking way I could tell them cops that I had been shot while being robbed of money to pay for a hit man to kill my wife.

The ambulance finally arrived, and the EMTs rushed over to me. They began feeling me up for vitals, putting blood pressure cuffs on me. "Start a line! He has lost a lot of blood!" one of the EMTs yelled. I was quickly rolled onto a gurney and worked on. Before they hoisted me up off the floor, I already had an IV line started, an oxygen mask over my face, and I was wrapped in sterile sheets with nothing exposed but my face.

I was praying they would give me something to make me black out. The pain that ripped through my body was unbearable now. My entire body hurt with every pump of my heart.

I was being rolled out of the bloodied hotel room when I overheard some of the cops who were standing around talking. "This has been a bloody fucking day in Virginia Beach," a tall black cop said. "I just came on shift and already heard about a pregnant woman being shot up in her car. Fucking tragic. I don't know who would do some shit like that to a woman about to give birth."

I squeezed my eyes closed even tighter. I felt more pain erupt in my chest. I knew they were speaking about Trice. I was trying very hard to hear if they would say whether or not she lived.

"A coward, that's who," a different cop chimed in. "That case already has national attention, and trust me, the two detectives they have working it are damn good."

"I hope they get the motherfucker who did it and who set the whole thing up," the tall black cop replied. "I'm hearing they think it was a murder-for-hire hit. Probably the low-down dirty husband . . . another fucking Rae Carruth or

Scott Peterson in our own fucking backyard. I will do what I can to help bring that bastard down so they can fry his fucking balls."

The cops weren't talking directly to me, but it seemed like they were. I felt a strong sense of guilt trampling over me. I was praying that God would knock me unconscious so I wouldn't have to listen to this shit. I guess it was meant for me to suffer with this pain and guilt. I couldn't help but think of Trice as they lifted me into the back of the ambulance. I never really wanted her to die. I was overcome with anger, hurt, and feelings of betrayal. I wasn't the *murder-for-hire* type. I wasn't a psychopath like Scott Peterson, who cold-bloodedly killed his wife and unborn child. At least, I didn't think of myself as that kind of monster. I guess I really was. Instead of walking away from a cheating wife, I chose to have her and that unborn bastard child killed.

Charlene didn't help matters either. I was so stupid to let her make me believe she ever really cared about me. She just wanted revenge. I hope my friend Doug had followed me to the hotel like I had asked him to. I told him to watch Charlene's car and if he saw Charlene leave the hotel without me, to follow her until he heard from me. I told him if he didn't hear from me in more than two hours, to come back to the hotel and call the police, because it meant I was probably tied up, beaten up, or, worse, dead. I never told Doug exactly what it was all about; I just told him to trust me on this one and do as I asked.

As the ambulance turned into the hospital's trauma center unloading bay, I was praying the whole time that Doug had kept track of Charlene. If I lived through this, Charlene was going to pay dearly for everything that she'd done. She wouldn't get away scot-free with taking my money and destroying all those lives she had left in her wake. I still hadn't forgotten that she was the cause of all this controversy in the first damn place.

One lie told by a scorned wife destroyed four lives like a stack of dominos falling.

"Male gunshot victim! Lost a lot of blood but seems to be fighting through it. Must be the will of God that he is still alive!" one of the EMTs relayed to the hospital's trauma staff as they whirled around me in a frenzy to save my life.

"Sometimes we don't understand it all, but God must have a divine purpose for this one, because he should've been dead hours ago," a nurse said as she probed my body with her hands.

"Prep for surgery . . . it won't be much longer if we don't get him to surgery!" someone else said from the side of me. I just closed my eyes and asked God that His will be done. If I came out of this alive, I was definitely going to fulfill my purpose.

27

Trice

When I woke up from the heavy sedatives, my head was pounding and my mouth was so dry and pasty, it felt as if I'd eaten a jar of Elmer's Art Paste. The first person I saw when I cracked my eyes open was Dr. Jackson. He was scribbling on the clipboard that hung from the foot of the bed. He noticed me watching him and cracked a smile. I rolled my eyes at him. There was nothing to smile about. Here I was lying all fucked up in a hospital bed, and I quickly remembered that he was the one who had broken the bad news to me about my baby.

I pulled the oxygen cannula out of my nose. I no longer had the breathing tube, which I guess was a good sign. I didn't even know how long I'd been knocked out. Dr. Jackson walked over to the side of the bed, still flashing that stupid little grin.

"Hello, Mrs. Davis, glad you could join us." He smirked.

I guess he thought he was being funny or comforting, but I wanted to curse his ass out. I didn't know on whom to direct the overwhelming anger I felt, but somebody somewhere had to get the wrath.

"Are you in a lot of pain? If you are, we can give you some more sedatives to make you comfortable. You've made strides in the past two days," he said, looking down at me like I was a pitiful case. I shook my head no to the sedatives. There was only so much sleeping and feeling loopy I could take. I wanted to deal with the issues at hand.

"That's fine. When you're feeling stronger, we'll talk more," Dr. Jackson said. He patted my arm and turned to walk out the door.

"Wait," I rasped, my voice strained and coming out in a grating whisper. Dr. Jackson whirled around on his heels and smiled as he walked back over to the side of my bed.

"Oh, Mrs. Davis, it is so nice to hear you get enough air into those lungs to speak. You are definitely going to make a recovery. You had us a little worried there for a minute," he chimed.

He was too fucking happy-go-lucky for me. I rolled my eyes and moved my head in frustration. My words were all jumbled up in my brain, and it seemed like my fucking tongue didn't want to cooperate. I opened my mouth to speak, but it was taking a while to get the thoughts out.

"What? What is it?" he asked, touching my arm again. "Take your time."

"My baby? The . . . the . . . detectives?" I managed. Getting those few words to come out had sapped all of my energy just that fast. I exhaled in frustration. Dr. Jackson looked at me like he understood just what I was asking.

"The baby is still in the morgue. We wanted to give you the opportunity to do a proper burial since your daughter was full term. Yes, there were detectives here to see you, but I asked them to leave. You were in no condition to be questioned. There is a big investigation going on in Virginia Beach about you, young lady," Dr. Jackson informed me. I looked at him quizzically. He nodded.

"Oh, yeah, everyone is wondering who would do such a horrific thing to a woman about to give birth. It has made almost every national paper. I think every investigative bureau is involved too. They say whoever shot you was definitely trying to kill you and the baby. The question is *why*," Dr. Jackson continued.

Tears sprang to my eyes. I could remember some of what happened, and things started to flash in my head. I remembered the phone call I received just before it all happened, the man on the motorcycle and how he had followed me, and then, the most important thing, a flash of lightning.

I couldn't believe everything that had happened. My mind was somewhat functioning now. I was still thinking back on that moment. The guy was saying something before he shot me. What was it? Oh, shit! He was yelling, "This is from your husband," right before he started shooting. *Troy, how could you? How could you kill our child?*

My heart started to race as I listened to Dr. Jackson recount things that had obviously been pushed to the back of my mind in light of my condition. I reached out and touched his hand to shut him up. I had something to say, and I knew it would take a few minutes for my tongue to connect with my brain. He paused and looked at me. My eyes were moving rapidly, because I was so upset. The heart monitors were going crazy beeping and ringing. Dr. Jackson's face registered alarm.

"Mrs. Davis . . . I didn't mean to upset you. I don't want to set you back now. Please, take your time and rest," he said. The sounds of the heart monitors had drawn two more doctors and three nurses into my room. I was flailing my arms wildly. Finally the words came to my mouth.

"I know who . . . who . . . tried to . . . kill . . . me," I gasped, still moving my hands. My words gave everyone in the room pause. There were at least six sets of eyes on me, and I could feel the heat of their gazes. I was a national phenomenon and everyone wanted to know who had tried to kill the poor pregnant woman and her unborn baby. I relaxed my body so that my words would be loud and clear in that room. No one said a word as if they wanted to make sure I could be heard.

"It . . . it . . . was my . . . husband. My husband killed . . . our . . . our baby and he wanted me . . . dead." I struggled with each word, but they all came out just the same. I heard one nurse gasp. Some of the others looked at each other in shock. Dr. Jackson's face went stony as if he was so angry he could find Troy and kill him with his bare hands.

"Somebody go call those detectives back in here, now!" Dr. Jackson barked. The nurses and other doctors were moving slowly. I guess they were still in utter shock. "Now! Get on the phones now!" Dr. Jackson followed up. He touched my arm gently. "Trust me . . . your husband won't get away with what he did. I'm so glad you lived to tell the story," Dr. Jackson said, his voice soothing and calming.

I just closed my eyes. I was glad I had lived to tell the story too. Troy was going to pay for what he had done. I was going to make sure of that.

28

Charlene

Leon Jr. and I had been in Delaware for two days. He was begging me to take him to Chuck E. Cheese's, and I wanted to do some shopping at the Christiana Mall. I had heard so much about the mall that I had to check it out.

It was the end of the second day, and I decided it was time for me to get the hell on. I returned to the hotel, loaded down with bags from shopping. When I went into the room, I noticed the *Newsday* paper under the door. I kicked it inside and went to pick it up and drop it in the pile with the other day's papers. When I set my bags down and grabbed the paper, my heart almost stopped beating. I clasped my hand over my mouth when I saw the picture and the caption:

VIRGINIA BEACH WOMAN VICTIM OF A MURDER FOR HIRE SURVIVES, UNBORN BABY DEAD, HUSBAND PRIME SUSPECT

I flopped down in the chair and gripped the newspaper tightly in my hands. I kept staring at the caption and the side-by-side pictures of Trice and Troy. Although I knew it was going to happen, the shit really didn't hit home until I saw this. I shook my head and began reading the article. I couldn't read the shit fast enough to find out if Troy was alive too. I was scanning fast. Certain phrases were jumping out at me.

Woman survives brutal shooting on the way to the hospital to give birth. Fetus does not survive. This shit was crazy. How in the fuck did the hit man not finish the damn job? Next I read, *Mrs. Davis awakens from coma to tell doctors that her husband tried to have her killed for a newly drawn up insurance policy that he forcibly made her sign just seven weeks ago.*

I shook my head. That bitch Trice must be like a fucking cat with nine fucking lives. She had now survived two fucking shootings. Where does shit like that happen besides movies and fiction books? I had an instant fucking headache. Good thing I had purchased a new cell phone. I needed to call Delsey right away to find out the rumblings in Virginia Beach.

You know, the streets always had the story more correct than any newspaper or media outlet.

My son started bugging me to open some of the toys we'd gotten at Toys "R" Us. "Russell! Don't bother me right now! Do what you want to do!" I barked at him.

I was immediately sorry, but I was preoccupied. I went into our bathroom and dialed Delsey. My legs were rocking back and forth so hard and fast from my nerves being on edge. "Come on, bitch, answer the phone. I know it's a strange number, but answer the goddamn phone," I huffed under my breath. Finally, I heard Delsey's voice on the line.

"Girl! It's Charlene, I need to talk to you," I rushed out my words. Delsey was quiet for a minute. Then she smacked her lips like she was annoyed.

"Charlene, did you steal my driver's license?" Delsey snapped. That shit just sent me over the top with anger.

"What? I don't have to steal your license, Delsey! I have more important, pressing things on my mind!" I retorted. She seemed to calm down.

"I called to see if you picked up all the mail from my apartment, and I wanted to find out what is being said on the streets of Norfolk and Virginia Beach about the shooting involving Trice and Troy Davis," I rambled, my words coming fast and furious.

"I got your mail. There is a letter from the prison. It says 'to the wife of Leon Bunch,'" Delsey told me.

"Ugh, open it up," I instructed. I figured it was going to be a letter telling me his ass was in the infirmary or some shit.

Delsey began reading it.

Dear Mrs. Bunch, we have tried several times to contact you in person. We are writing to inform you of the untimely death of your spouse, Mr. Leon Bunch. Please contact—

"What? Dead?" I shouted, cutting Delsey off. It felt like the wind had been let out of my lungs. I didn't tell those bastards to kill Leon. I just wanted him to be hurt real bad. I held my head in my hands. I expected a deluge of tears to come falling, but for some evil damn reason I couldn't muster up any tears to shed for that nigga.

"I'm sorry, girl," Delsey said solemnly. "I can only imagine what them COs let happen to Leon. That's a damn shame."

I had to at least act like I was sniffling.

"And about that story of Trice and Troy. Girl, they are saying that Troy hired a hit man to kill Trice, because he wanted to collect insurance money. But get this shit—guess who he hired?" Delsey told me and asked all in one breath.

"Who?" I asked, acting dumb.

"Girl, your fucking cousin Dray! Yes, ma'am!" Delsey relayed like the world's biggest gossip.

"What? How you figure that?" I asked, probing deeper.

"Because the word on the street is Dray shot Troy when Troy didn't have the money, and when Dray realized the cops were coming to get his ass, he shot himself in the head. Charlene, I'm sorry to say that your cousin is dead too."

My eyes shot open wide. My pulse sped up. "So Troy is alive?" I asked, concern lacing my words.

"Huh? Why is you asking about that nigga? I just told you your cousin is dead," Delsey said suspiciously.

"I am just trying to figure out how all of this went down," I replied sassily.

"Well, yeah, Troy is supposed to be alive. He is in the same damn hospital as his wife, who he almost killed. Ain't that some shit out of the movies?" Delsey said.

"Yeah, girl. I have to go now. Please don't give anyone this phone number. I have to deal with Leon and Dray being gone. It is all just too much," I faked concern.

"Okay. Well, good luck up north," Delsey replied. My heart automatically seized in my chest.

"Who told you I was going up north?" I asked in an alarmed tone. Delsey started stuttering. "Delsey! Who the fuck told you anything about where I was headed?" I snapped. "Hello? Hello?" I called out. The line was dead. Delsey had hung up on me. Panic struck my ass like a ten-ton boulder. I threw that fucking cell phone down in the bathroom sink and raced into the room with Leon Jr.

"Come on, baby, we have to go!" I shouted to my son as I raced around trying to gather up a few of the things we had just bought. I opened the hotel room safe and unloaded my cash back into the duffel bag. My son was still sitting on the floor playing.

"Come on, I said! We have to go! The game here is over. We have to run to our car like we are racing, okay?" I said to him.

Once again, we were on the run. I didn't know who Delsey had been speaking to, and I didn't know how the fuck she knew I was headed north, but I did know that a change of fucking plans was in order. Something was amiss, and I wasn't sticking around to find out what. I was thinking hard about how I could change the course of my destination.

When I got to my car, I was sweating and out of breath, and my son was all-out bawling from having to leave behind some of his new toys. As stressed out as I was, I wanted to yank his little ass up and tell him to shut the fuck up. But I realized just like I was stressed, so was my poor baby.

I was starting to think this fucking fifty thousand dollars might not have been worth all of this, especially uprooting my child. His friends and what little family he had were in the Norfolk/Virginia Beach area. That's all he knew. But it was too late.

I was already dead in the middle of this shit, so I had to work on getting myself together. I raced around to the trunk and dumped all of the bags inside. I put my crying son in the car, secured the seat belt, kissed his head, and went to the driver's side. Before I could sit down in the car, I noticed a note on my windshield. "What the fuck is that?" I growled. I put my leg back out of the car and snatched the paper off the window. It was a note written in the most horrible handwriting I had ever seen in my life.

I know everything you did. I have been watching you since you got here. You can't see me, but I can see you. Everything you did in Virginia is going to follow you forever. You'll hear from me again soon.

My hands were trembling so hard I could hardly keep a grip on the thick piece of paper. I felt like throwing the fuck up. My chest heaved up and down and I had to keep myself from fainting. I was scared shitless. I couldn't even front on that.

I finally got behind the steering wheel of the car. My eyes frantically darted around the hotel parking lot, looking for someone who might be watching me. It was dead as ever. I couldn't see anyone. There were a bunch of cars coming in and going out of the lot, since the place was in such a busy area. There was no telling who had left that note.

Calling Delsey and then finding this note made me that much more paranoid. It was all too fucking much to think about. I put my car in drive and began pulling out of the lot. I was trying my best to watch my surroundings for any suspicious-looking vehicles. Nothing. As I got to the stop sign to ease out of the lot, I looked in my rearview mirror. There were at least four cars lined up to pull out behind me.

"Fuck!" I whispered as I stared out the back window. The car directly behind me blared its horn, telling me to move my ass. I snapped out of it and pulled onto the road. All of the cars pulled out as well. There was no telling which one was following me. I looked ahead and there were two signs, one pointing north and one pointing south.

I was confused as to which direction to go.

I thought I had come out on top.

Maybe not.

29

Troy

I was thrust out of my sleep by the pain radiating through my entire body, but especially in the lower half of my extremities. I moved my head left to right and blinked against the bright lights. I realized I was in a hospital room. I closed my eyes again when I realized I wasn't dreaming and I wasn't dead. Instead, I was still alive and dealing with pain. They had saved my life.

Those fucking doctors rushed me into surgery, which I vaguely remembered, when I arrived at the emergency room, and apparently they had worked to save my trifling-ass life. I was actually feeling angry and upset that I could feel anything at all. When the police kicked into the hotel room, I wanted to fucking die. I know I had begged Dray to get me some help so I could live, but that was when I still had that insurance money on my mind. Since then I just wanted the grim reaper to come and snatch my ass away from this world. I had done something fucked up and I deserved to die.

I guess it had been a couple of days since the shooting and my surgery. Although I was awake, I was pretty drowsy. I didn't remember a damn thing from the last two days. I guess the medical staff had kept me heavily sedated. Probably so I wouldn't be in pain all the damn time. The last thing I remembered was being rushed into surgery.

My eyes darted around the room and stopped near the door. I was being guarded by two uniformed police officers. I squinted in confusion. My initial thought was maybe they were protecting me from whoever they thought shot me. Then I looked around and noticed a nurse changing something on my monitors. She noticed my eyes were open and she kind of did a double take like she hadn't expected to see me alive again.

I opened my mouth, but no words came out. Her facial expression quickly changed from surprise to see me awake to a frown mixed with a scowl. The nurse looked down at me with disdain and shook her head like she was disgusted to see me alive. Then she turned toward the officers and said, "I think you officers wanted to know when he opened his eyes. I guess this means he's going to make it," the nurse droned as if she was mad at me for surviving my gunshot wound.

The two officers seemed to snap to life. They dropped whatever it was they were doing and zoomed in on me. They both walked over to see for themselves that I was actually awake. They both looked down at me for confirmation and then they looked at each other. Damn. From their facial expressions, it was as if they were seeing a damn ghost or something.

"We better call Detective Grantham right away before something changes," one of the officers said to the other.

"Yeah, he'll want to get here right away. You never know how these things can turn out," the other officer replied.

They both went for their radios at the same time. They were like Keystone cops tripping over one another to be the first to make the call to contact the detective. A feeling of dread washed over me. I didn't know why they were so gung ho to get the detective to come see me. My mind was still kind of muddled from the sedatives and deep sleep. I was trying to get my thoughts together. Since a detective would be talking to me soon, I needed to get myself together sooner rather than later.

All kinds of mixed emotions were running through my head. I suddenly remembered the story I was prepared to tell the police if they asked how and why I had been shot. I exhaled when I remembered I had planned to tell the police Dray shot me when we got into an argument and then shot himself when he thought he was going back to prison. I didn't care if they even thought Dray and I were lovers or anything. I just didn't want them to know the damn truth.

I started feeling better about the cops being there, despite the pain that was racking my lower abdomen. After the call went out to Detective Grantham, the radio traffic exploded. It was like pandemonium had erupted over the cops' radio frequency.

The nurse stared at both of the officers. She shook her head like a teacher about to chastise her students. "I know this is an important case, but I'm going to have to ask both of you to wait outside. I mean, I understand the circumstances, but he is still unfortunately my patient and I have to adhere to the hospital's rules about disturbing the patients," she stated.

The officers didn't complain or object. They strolled outside the room, and for that moment it became unbelievably peaceful.

"You would have been better off dead with what they have on you," the nurse turned to me and hissed. I stared at her, confused. "Hmph, I personally hope they give you the chair for what you did. It is only because of the Christian in me that I can even stand to take care of the likes of you." Then she took one last look at me with a disgusted scowl painting her face, turned, and stomped out of the room.

My mind raced with questions. It was impossible for them to know what I had done. I was sure Trice had been killed, so who would that leave to tell the cops anything about what I had done? I was certain it wasn't Charlene. No way she would implicate herself for shooting me, hiring a hit man, and indirectly causing Dray's death. I closed my eyes, exhausted from my thoughts. My questions would soon be answered.

I didn't know how long it had been since the two officers called the detective. I do know I was fighting sleep when Detective Grantham walked in. He was a huge black man, with square shoulders and a mean, ugly-ass mug. He casually walked over to my bed. I kept my eyes on him and he looked down at me for what seemed like an eternity.

"Mr. Davis, I am Detective Grantham. Can you understand what I am saying to you?" he asked. His voice boomed with a lot of bass. How could I not hear what he was saying to me? This was about ensuring I was lucid enough to answer questions and incriminate myself. I nodded, which may have been my first mistake.

"Do you think you can talk to me about some things that have happened over the past week?" he asked. If you ask any cop or detective what was the biggest thing hindering their job today, every one of them would answer the same: "TV shows like *Law and Order* and *CSI.*" It made criminals think they were smart and knew the law. Detective Grantham should have never asked because I wasn't about to answer any questions without a lawyer. And yes, I had seen my share of cop shows to know I did have rights. And the first of those rights was the right to an attorney. I wasn't that out of it to exercise my right. I shook my head in the negative to signal that I was saying no to his question.

"So you don't want to talk to me about how your pregnant wife got shot and how your baby ended up dead?" Detective Grantham boomed. The man was cool, which probably added to his reputation as being the best. I shook my head again. Detective Grantham began flexing his jaw rapidly. I think if I wasn't in the ICU, where the nurses and doctors were so close, he would have tried to inflict some real serious police brutality on my ass.

"Well, maybe this will help you change your mind, Mr. Davis," Detective Grantham said. He held a Polaroid picture in front of my face. It was so close I couldn't help but look at it. A feeling of dread washed over me as I stared at the dead baby. Her face was curled like she had been in pain when she died, and as I stared at her, I could see nothing but me. She was all me—nose, eyes, lips. I didn't think I had ever seen a newborn come out looking so much like one parent. My heart began pounding so hard I thought it would jump out of my chest. Tears sprang up in my eyes immediately.

Detective Grantham finally moved the picture away. "Still won't change your mind?" he growled. Then he put another picture in front of my face. It was a picture of Trice. She was all bloodied on a surgical table and the doctors were working on her to save her life. I closed my eyes after looking at that one. Tears were flowing fast from my eyes now.

"So, tell me, Mr. Davis . . . you still don't want to talk to me about what happened to your wife and your baby daughter?" He was leaning over me so close his breath was hot on my face. "I know what you did. I know all about the insurance. I know you got someone to shoot your wife. And the best thing of all is your wife survived. She is going to testify against you, and you don't stand a snowball's chance in hell to get out of this one. I guess you wish you'd died in that hotel room, but God made sure that you lived to face the consequences of killing that innocent little baby . . . your fucking baby," Detective Grantham said through clenched teeth.

I squeezed my eyes shut, and I couldn't control myself anymore. I was a fucking monster. I deserved to rot in hell. I had commissioned the death of my own baby. I couldn't even describe the feeling that rocked through my body.

"Aggghhhh!" I screamed. It took everything I

had inside of me to get that scream out. I lifted my hands and began banging on the bed rails. "Aggghh!" It hurt so bad and the emotional pain was killing me. My screams brought many from the medical staff to my room. Some of the doctors and nurses actually came into my room, others just buzzed around the door. I heard a couple of doctors say that I needed a sedative.

"That's enough, Detective," my regular nurse said.

I also saw the two uniformed police officers at the door. They had disappeared while Detective Grantham questioned me. They were all looking at me as if I had lost my mind. They were absolutely right. I felt as if I were losing my mind. It was all too much to bear.

"Detective, I am going to have to ask you to leave now," a small Asian doctor said to Grantham.

"Not before I read this heartless bastard his rights. In case all of you health professionals didn't know, this man is under arrest for the murder of his unborn daughter and the attempted murder of his wife," Detective Grantham announced. He nodded to the police officers, who approached me.

"Get the fuck away from me!" I belted out as I flailed my arms.

"We will, as soon as we cuff you to this bed," one of the officers snapped.

My arms were grabbed roughly and forced down. I felt the cold steel of the handcuffs clash with my skin. Next, I saw and heard the metal from the cuffs and the metal from the bed clash together with a loud clang. My other hand was released. Detective Grantham had an evil little grin on his face when he stepped back over to the bedside.

"Mr. Davis, you are under arrest for the murder of your baby daughter and the attempted murder of your wife, Trice Davis. You have the right to remain silent, anything you say can and will be held against you. You have the right to an attorney . . ."

My ears were ringing now. I knew if I didn't get the right attorney, I would never see the light of day again. Hell, I was guilty, but in a court of law I was innocent until proven guilty. Yeah, I felt like shit. I wanted and needed forgiveness. And as much as I wanted to apologize to Trice, I wished I had never met her ass. She deceived me. She fell in love with another man and instead of letting me go, she lied to me and tried to play me. She played me for a weakling. Now our baby was dead, she had survived more bullets, and in all likelihood, I was spending my remaining days incarcerated.

And regardless of how fucked up everything was, all I wanted was an opportunity to tell Trice that I was sorry, that I had made a grave mistake.

I wanted to rot in hell for what I had done to my own baby.

30

Trice

When the detective showed up in my hospital room, it really hit me. Reality slapped me in the face with the strength of a gorilla's hand. It hurt too. Things started flashing in front of my eyes. I began to think back when Troy threw insurance papers at me and forced me to sign them. Then he disappeared all times of the day and night. Money started disappearing from our accounts and then to add insult to injury, Troy later took my name off our accounts. He also stalled me at the house the day I was shot. What a coincidence that was! But guess what? It wasn't a coincidence. And now I knew that Troy tried to kill me. Those words wouldn't stop ringing in my head now that I was awake and coherent.

Troy tried to kill me. Troy tried to kill me. Troy tried to kill me, I chanted repeatedly in my head.

It was hard for me to not put blame on me. *What if I never cheated with Leon? What if I had been a better wife? What if I hadn't visited Leon repeatedly at the prison, behind Troy's back, thinking Leon was my unborn child's baby daddy? What if I hadn't been dick crazy? What if I had just gone to the hospital instead of waiting for Troy?*

I had caused all of this, but I didn't care. He had many opportunities to just walk away. He could have filed for divorce, asked for a paternity test, anything, except kill my child. There was no way I was going to blame myself for any of this.

When Dr. Jackson made the call, only one detective showed up. He had rushed over to my bedside and extended his hand for me to shake. I barely lifted my hand to meet his.

Dr. Jackson stayed with me the entire time. He stood on my right side, while the detective stood on my left side. I sized him up and he did the same.

"Mrs. Davis, I'm Detective Grantham. I'm glad to see that you made it," he said in a nice mannerly tone. I cracked a halfhearted smile.

"We understand that you may have some information you want to share with us," he said.

I nodded. He looked at me expectantly. I planned on giving him the whole truth—everything about the *Trading Spouses* show, my affair with Leon, and Troy's thing with Charlene. I wanted him to know that Troy had motive to have me killed.

"I know my husband tried to have me killed for insurance money," I began. "The man on the motorcycle who shot me said it had come from my husband. But I received a call before I left the house, and I think it came from a girl named Charlene. You see . . . we all went on a show called *Trading Spouses*," I began.

Detective Grantham's and Dr. Jackson's gazes were fixed on me. They were hanging on my every word as I ran it all down. I left no stone unturned. In the end, my daughter was dead and I had nothing to lose. Before the detective had arrived, Dr. Jackson had told me I had suffered too much damage to my uterus, so they had to perform a hysterectomy. That meant I had no uterus and no chances of ever getting pregnant again. *What man would ever want me?* Troy had officially ruined my life in the worst way possible.

When I finished telling them the story, Detective Grantham informed me Troy was in the same hospital. He said someone had shot Troy. The police thought Troy had been shot after he went to pay for the hit but that one other guy, a known criminal, was found dead. They were still trying to figure out exactly what happened, but they believed my story.

"I assure you, Mrs. Davis, your husband will be

brought to justice for what he has done to you and your baby," Detective Grantham promised.

He and I had a few more exchanges and then he left. That Q & A session the detective and I had definitely put my mind at ease. And after Dr. Jackson left my room, I was able to get some rest.

The following morning, Dr. Jackson walked into my room and told me that Detective Grantham, along with another detective, just served Troy with an arrest warrant. "They have him handcuffed to his bed right now," he said.

"So they're taking him out of the hospital right now?" I asked. The thought of Troy getting his just deserts was like music to my ears. I only wished that I could see his ass while they were escorting him out of the hospital.

"No. They can't take him anywhere until he's discharged. And that isn't likely to happen for another day or so. There's gonna be a police officer standing guard while he's under hospital care," Dr. Jackson explained.

"If I was able to see him right now, I would laugh at him and spit right in his face," I said, getting emotional. The thought of what he did to me was beginning to get underneath my skin.

Dr. Jackson massaged my left shoulder. "Calm down. Believe me, he's going to get what's coming to him."

Dr. Jackson was a trauma doctor, but even after I was moved to a regular ward, he still came by to see me every day. I figured he did it because of the death of my baby. He knew I took the loss to heart. He was definitely a caring man, and he was a gift from God. And on my final day at the hospital, he made sure I had everything I needed. He even made sure my sister Anna was there after I was discharged. And in return, I promised to keep in close contact with him.

On my way out of the hospital, Anna expressed how much she loved me and how well I looked despite everything I had been through. But then after she drove away from the hospital, she and I got into a conversation about the loss of my baby and my feelings regarding Troy.

"Anna, I just want to bury my baby and put all this mess behind me. And as far as Troy is concerned, I am confident the police will take care of him," I replied to her softly.

"I know, sis, I know," Anna said sympathetically.

I remained quiet and thought about how I got to this place in my life. I admit that I played with fire going between Troy and Leon, and in the end, my baby was the one who got burned. I wished I had come clean with Troy—my daughter would be alive now. She would have a father who loved her, whether we were together or not, and me, her mom, who would have been there for her all of her days. In the end, Leon showed his true colors. I played the wrong cards choosing Leon over Troy, and now I wished I could trade places with her.

Right after I helped the police put Troy away for life.

31

Charlene

That bitch Delsey called my phone again, and I didn't answer. I had been driving like a bat out of hell after I received that note on my car, and I didn't have time to fuck around with her ass. I saw that she left a message, but I didn't try to retrieve it while I was driving. I had Leon Jr. in the car, and I had getting someplace safe on my mind.

I finally decided to go to Florida. So that meant I had driven all the way to Delaware for nothing. Now that Delsey and probably the whole neighborhood knew I was going north, I switched it up and went south. But that meant I had to drive back through Virginia. I set my GPS to take me on a route that didn't require me to go through my hometown.

I was exhausted by the time I crossed the North Carolina state line. I had been concentrating on driving, along with keeping my son from driving me crazy and trying to figure out if someone was following me. It was nearly impossible to keep track of all of the different cars on the interstate. Shit, I couldn't believe the number of black trucks I'd seen that looked just like Dray's Tahoe or how many cars resembled Troy's. There was no telling who could've been tailing me.

"Baby, we are stopping at this gas station and Mommy is going to get you some food, okay?" I said to Leon Jr. He was half asleep, but he moaned his agreement. I eased the car into a Wawa gas station because I knew Wawa sold good breakfast and lunch. I could get us something to eat now and something to have in the car for later. I wasn't planning on stopping again after this until I landed my ass in Fort Lauderdale or Miami.

I got out of the car and slid a dark pair of Gucci shades over my eyes. They were just one of the things I was able to cop in Delaware before I ran the hell away from there. I looked around to make sure I didn't notice anyone watching me. Shit, it was too hard to tell with all the cars at the gas station. There were five or six people getting gas; they didn't seem interested in me. Then there were people parked, getting out of cars to go into the store, and some leaving. It was just too much traffic in and out to be sure. I shrugged and told myself I was being crazy right now. I was beyond paranoid. Maybe someone had just left that fucking note on my car to be cruel. I grabbed my son out of the car.

"Come on. We're going to the bathroom, getting some food and gas, and getting out of here. How would you like to go to Disney World?!" I told him excitedly.

"Yeah!" he screamed.

We walked inside the Wawa hand in hand. I ordered our food and then took him to the bathroom. I relieved myself as well. When I came out, I noticed a young guy standing by the door. In fact, my son and I ran right into him.

"Oh, excuse me! You scared me," I exclaimed, holding my chest. He wasn't someone I had seen before, so I felt a little better about that. I didn't know why his ass was standing right outside the door like that when there was room in front of the men's bathroom. The guy gave me a funny look, but he didn't say a word. I pulled my son along.

"Come on, we have to go," I said. I grabbed some juices, sodas, and waters and rushed over to the counter.

"Fill it up on pump six," I said to the woman behind the counter. This fat redneck had a cigarette hanging out of her mouth, and she was moving slow as fucking molasses through a straw. I blew a long breath out of my nose and tapped my foot as I waited for this lazy bitch to ring up my stuff. As I waited, I noticed out of my peripheral vision that the same creepy-ass guy had come out of the bathroom. He was looking at me, which unnerved me.

"Can you speed it up?" I asked the fat, nasty clerk. She grunted like the pig that she was and finally put my shit in the bag and gave me my total. I threw the money up on the counter, grabbed my son's hand, and rushed out the door.

I ran to my car, put my son inside, and started pumping the gas. That fucking gas could not come out fast enough. I was squeezing the pump like my life depended on it. I looked through the glass window of the Wawa and I didn't see the strange guy anymore.

"Okay, Charlene . . . bitch, stop bugging the fuck out thinking everybody is after you," I mumbled to myself. I had to kind of chuckle to myself. I was really thinking that motherfucker was coming outside to get my ass. Finally, my car was full of gas. I had a second wind and I had about three Red Bulls and a cup of coffee in my car. I got back into my car, started it up, and checked on my son one last time before I pulled out.

"You good, baby boy?" I asked. He nodded his head up and down because his mouth was too full of food to answer. "Greedy self," I joked. I eased the car toward the exit and turned my radio up. "Oh, shit, wait," I said. I stopped for a second and got my cell phone. I wanted to listen to the message Delsey had left for me as I waited in line to pull out onto the street.

"Charlene, this is Delsey. I just wanted to tell you that you got an entire city looking for your ass. The police are looking for you because I heard that you paid some guy to beat up Leon, but they killed him. Some of Dray's boys are looking for you, too, because they said you beat them out of some money and caused Dray to commit suicide. Then I heard you was part of that big case against Troy. And Troy is singing like a bird. He told the cops you set up the entire hit on Trice, but you took the hit money and ran. Girl, there are at least two APBs out for you and half the hood looking for you. You better not never come back to Norfolk or the Tidewater area period."

I couldn't front. That message chilled me to the bone. Here I was thinking I had gotten out of Norfolk free and clear. I tossed my phone onto the passenger seat and tried to clear my mind. It was my turn to pull onto the street, and just as I eased my foot onto the gas I was startled.

"Aghh! What the fuck are you doing?" I

screamed, slamming on my brakes. A white van had stopped abruptly in front of me, causing me to almost run right into it. "Move your fucking car!" I screamed, leaning on my horn. The next thing I knew, the side door of the van slid open and three masked men jumped out.

"Oh my God! Baby!" I shrieked. All I could think about was my son as the cats bum-rushed my car. There was no place for me to run or go. Everything else seemed to happen in slow fucking motion. My door was yanked open and I was yanked out of the car. A large, leather-gloved hand was placed over my nose and mouth so I couldn't even scream. My face was covered so much that I couldn't see what was happening to my son. I tried to kick and fight, but I was no match for whoever was snatching me. I could feel myself being carried away. In my head I was screaming at the top of my lungs, but only muffled moans escaped my lips.

"You thought you were fucking with amateurs, huh? You can't take niggas' money and run and think it's all good," a man hissed in my ear as I was forcefully thrown into the van. There were no seats in the back of the van. A black hood was quickly thrown over my head, so I couldn't see any faces. There were at least four different voices. That much I could tell. The inside of the van smelled heavily of weed and liquor. The floor was cold, so they must've taken the carpet up out of the van too.

When I heard the door slam, I felt like someone had shot me. All I could think was that they were going to take me to some remote area someplace and shoot my ass right in the head.

"Please! Just don't hurt my son!" I cried out.

The next thing I felt was a sharp pain around my head.

"Agh!" I belted out. "I'll give you anything you want. Please, the money is in the trunk of the car. I only spent about three thousand . . . you can have the rest. Just please don't hurt my son," I kept on begging. I couldn't give up that easily.

Another grating pain slammed into the center of my face. Crack. Slap. Punch. I was fielding blow after blow to my head and face through the black hood. I could barely keep my mouth open, but I wasn't giving up.

"Just don't hurt my baby . . . he is innocent," I rasped. I was sure my nose was broken as it gushed blood. The blood also ran into my mouth and down my throat. I took another hit that threatened to turn the lights out in my damn head.

"Shut up, bitch, before you get some more where that came from," a deep voice ordered. "If your fucking little boy dies, it's all your fault. You wanted to be a grimy bitch and this is the result of that. So remember, you'll have his blood on your hands if I decide to murk that little nigga."

I couldn't stop the tears and blood from

falling. I rocked back and forth and prayed fervently that they let Leon Jr. live. I prayed for my life as well, especially since I had no idea which of the people I had done dirty was sending this very bloody message of revenge.

32

Troy

I was released from the hospital straight to jail, where I would await my trial. When I received my bedside arraignment in the hospital, I had an attorney appointed to me. I was ready to just plead guilty, but my attorney told me not to. He told me to utilize my right to a trial.

When you're behind bars, word spreads like a forest fire. And it took no time at all to find out that Leon was dead. I was told that he died in prison at the hands of some niggas who beat the shit out of him. Charlene was wanted for questioning as the person responsible for Leon's death. He had died not knowing if Trice's baby was his. When I heard that part, it really didn't affect me because he was the reason behind the breakup of my marriage in the first place. I felt like he got what he deserved. My attorney told me we could possibly use that at the trial. He also informed me that we had to paint Trice as the evil bitch she had become, which wouldn't be too hard to do. She definitely showed me that there was another side to her ass.

Now, after my eighth week of sitting in jail, I received the motion of discovery report and found out that Trice was definitely going to testify against me at my trial. And when I read the part about Charlene having Leon killed, I couldn't do anything but shake my fucking head. Charlene was playing both sides of the fence. And if I ever got the chance to get my hands on her, she would be dead herself. But don't think I didn't have feelers out there for her ass too. She should be bound and gagged at this very moment. The niggas I had on the prowl promised they'd get the job done. So, in the end, she won't have a happy ending.

My trial day finally came, and I must say that I was mentally ready to take this thing head-on. Now, although my attorney was a court-appointed public defender, he was a fighter to say the least. I was dressed in a cheap polyester suit and horrible-looking tie, all of which had been provided by my attorney.

When I walked into that crowded-ass courtroom, my heart almost dropped into my toes. But nothing could have prepared me for the first time I saw Trice. My legs buckled and I almost fell to the floor. The guards who brought me in grabbed me and held me up.

Trice looked so beautiful. I was so stupid for what I had done to her. Her skin was so clear and flawless. Her hair hung long with a slight curl. She wore a dark suit and an even darker expression when she saw me. I could feel the hate emanating from her toward me. I hung my head low. I couldn't even look her in the eye. She had every right to hate me because I hated myself.

The judge called the court to order with three hard bangs of his gavel. I stood up as they stated the case against me, the *State of Virginia vs. Troy Davis*. The words hit me like a ton of bricks. I had never been in trouble in my life.

I sat through the trial like a zombie until the minute Trice was called to the stand. It was as if the world stood still. Her heels rang like gunshots on the hard courtroom floors. All of the spectators were silent, everyone waiting for the victim to tell her story. Trice raised her right hand and swore to tell the truth, the whole truth, and nothing but the truth. She stated her name for the record and sat down. I stared at her, but she didn't look at me at all. She stayed honed in on the district attorney and the new man in her life, who had been sitting next to her in the courtroom. I assumed he was the doctor my attorney told me about.

"Mrs. Davis, we'd like to thank you for being brave enough to come here today. We know it wasn't easy," the prosecutor said. My attorney began scribbling notes like crazy.

"Mrs. Davis, you were shot a few months ago, correct?" the prosecutor asked. Trice said yes in a low voice. The judge asked her to speak up. She nodded.

"At the time of the shooting, you were pregnant, correct?"

"Yes, sir, I was," Trice answered.

"Tell us what happened on the days leading up to the shooting and the day of the shooting if you will," the prosecutor said. Then he walked back over to his table, pulled out his chair, and sat down. Trice cleared her throat and dabbed at her eyes with a crumpled piece of tissue.

"Well, I just want to first say that my baby girl didn't make it. When I was shot, she was killed and never got the chance to live outside of my womb," Trice sobbed. Hushed moans and groans wafted throughout the courtroom. I couldn't take it anymore.

That part was hard to take. I wanted to break down, but I didn't, I couldn't. If I was destined for prison, I wasn't going in a punk who cried in court. That was the kiss of death and an invitation to be someone's bitch. Additionally, I had sympathy for Trice, but I was also realistic. Our daughter had died and she already had another man in her life. What kind of shit was that?

But I listened to her words, and I thought about the photograph the detective had shown me. She was my daughter. And she was dead. The shit between Trice, Leon, and me didn't matter. No one even cared. Like me, everyone in that courtroom was hanging on to Trice's every word. Her testimony didn't take long, but it felt like an eternity to me. Finally, they had gotten to the point where Trice would have to point me out.

"Mrs. Davis, you said that the man who shot you said the words 'this came from your husband.' Can you please point out for the court who your husband is?" the prosecutor asked.

It was the first time Trice and I had locked eyes since this entire ordeal started. She steeled herself and held her head up high. She took a deep breath, lifted her arm, extended her finger, and pointed in the direction of where I sat.

"That's my husband over there . . . Troy Davis. That's the man who ordered me dead," Trice said in a calm, stoic voice.

She knew she had just sealed my fate and sent me to prison for life.

33

Trice

Later that night, Anna thought it would be a good idea for her to stay with me at my house since I had a long day in court to be a witness for the prosecutor at Troy's trial. I was mentally drained thinking back on everything that had taken place in court earlier. And the look he gave me after the judge sentenced him to life in prison gave me chills. It was the exact same look he gave me on the night he choked me and made me sign the new insurance policy.

If he had the chance, I knew he'd kill me himself. Never mind the fact that he used to love me, because that was a dead issue. Troy still had hate in his heart for me and I sensed it. I just hoped that I could move beyond this tragedy and have a better life.

Meanwhile, I lay on my living room sofa and watched the late-night news. Anna sat in the lounge chair across from me and told me she had a few cravings and that she was about to head out to one of the convenience stores near my house. "Want me to pick you up some ice cream or chips while I'm out?" she asked me.

"No, I'm cool. But thanks," I told her.

"Are you sure? I mean, I haven't seen you eat anything all day. And you gotta eat something."

"I really don't have an appetite."

"Well, let me get you a cup of hot tea. That'll hold you."

"No. I'm fine. Really," I assured her.

Anna let out a long sigh. "Okay. Suit yourself. But if you change your mind, call me."

"Okay. I will."

She stood up from the lounge chair. "Mind if I wear your cute little Fendi ball cap? My hair looks a mess."

"Sure, I don't care. It's hanging on the doorknob of the closet right there by the front door," I told her.

I watched Anna retrieve my hat and place it on her head. "You look really cute sporting my hat."

"I know. So, I might just steal it," she replied, giving me the cheesiest smile she could muster up, and then she opened the front door.

I smiled back at her, but when I noticed there was a masked gunman at the front door with a gun pointed directly at Anna's head, I screamed. But it was too late. He had already pulled the trigger. *BOOM! BOOM!* I heard two rounds explode from the barrel of his gun and then he ran off. By this time, Anna had collapsed onto the floor and lay there motionless.

My heart raced against the time as I sprinted to the front door. I slammed it shut and locked it. I grabbed Anna's cell phone from her handbag and immediately dialed 911.

"Nine-one-one, what's your emergency?" a woman dispatcher answered.

"My sister was shot! Please send an ambulance quickly," I sobbed.

"Ma'am, where was she shot?"

"In the head," I managed to get out, while I tried to cradle Anna's head in my left arm.

"Is she breathing?"

"I don't think so. Please send somebody now," I begged and pleaded. The 911 operator instructed me to stay on the phone until help arrived.

I sat on the floor and rocked my sister back and forth and cried my poor heart out. I felt responsible for Anna's death because I knew that masked gunman was there to take me out. It just so happened that she was at the wrong place, at the wrong time.

"Do you know who shot your sister?" the 911 dispatcher continued to question me.

"No, but I know my husband Troy is behind it. He wants me dead! And he isn't gonna stop until it's done," I screamed through the phone, and then I looked down at my sister. And from that moment, I knew that I was living on borrowed time.

From *Fistful of Benjamins*
"Special Delivery" by Kiki Swinson
Available October 2014 wherever books
and ebooks are sold.

Prologue

"Oh my God, Eduardo. What do you think they will do to us? I don't want to die . . . I can't leave my son," I cried, barely able to get my words out between sobbing and the fact that my teeth were chattering together so badly.

The warehouse type of room we were being held captive in was freezing. I mean freezing like we were sitting inside of a meat locker type of freezing. I could even see puffs of frosty air with each breath that I took. I knew it was summertime outside, so the conditions inside where we were being held told me we were purposely being made to freeze. The smell of sawdust and industrial chemicals was also so strong that the combination was making my stomach churn. Eduardo flexed his back against mine and turned his head as much as the ropes that bound us together allowed. He was trembling from the subzero conditions as well.

"Gabby, just keep your mouth shut. If we gon' die right now, at least we are together. I know I ain't say it a lot, but I love you. I love you for everything you did and put up with from me. I am sorry I ever let you get into this bullshit from the jump. It wasn't no place for you from day one, baby girl," Eduardo whispered calmly through his battered lips.

With everything that had happened, I didn't know how he was staying so calm. It was like he had no emotion behind what was happening or like he had already resigned himself to the fact that we were dead. In my opinion, his ass should've been crying, fighting, and yelling for the scary men to let me go. Something. Eduardo was the drug dealer, not me, so maybe he had prepared himself to die many times. I hadn't ever prepared myself to die or to be tied up like an animal, beaten, and waiting to possibly get my head blown off. This was not how I saw my life ending up. All I had ever wanted was a good man, a happy family, a nice place to live, and just a good life.

"I don't care about being together when we die, Eduardo! You forget I have a son? Who is going to take care of him if I'm dead over something I didn't do?" I replied sharply. A pain shot through my skull like someone had shot me in the head. I was ready to lose it. My shoulders began quaking as I broke down in another round of sobs. I couldn't even feel the pain that had previously permeated my body from the beating I had taken. I was numb in comparison to the pain I was feeling in my heart behind leaving my son. I kept thinking about my son and my mother, who were probably both sitting in a strange place wondering how I had let this happen to them. That was the hard part, knowing that they were going to be innocent casualties of my stupid fucking actions. I should've stuck to carrying mail instead of stepping into the shit that had me in this predicament. I was the dummy in this situation. I was so busy looking for love in all the wrong places. I had done all of this to myself.

"Shhh. Don't cry. We just have to pray that Luca will have mercy on us. I will try to make him believe that it wasn't us. I'll tell him we didn't do it. We weren't responsible for everything that happened," Eduardo whispered to me.

"But he's the one who got us out so fast. I keep thinking that he only did that because he thought we might start talking. He got us out just so he could kill us, don't you see that? We are finished. Done. Dead," I said harshly. The tears were still coming. It was like Eduardo couldn't get what I was saying. We were both facing death and I wasn't ready to die!

"You don't know everything. Maybe it was something else. Let me handle—" Eduardo started to tell me, but his words were clipped short when we both heard the sound of footsteps moving toward us. The footsteps sounded off like gunshots against the icy cold concrete floors. My heart felt like it would explode through the bones in my chest, and suddenly it felt like my bladder was filled to capacity. The footsteps stopped. I think I stopped breathing too. Suddenly, I wasn't cold anymore. Maybe it was the adrenaline coursing fiercely through my veins, but suddenly I was burning up hot.

"Eduardo Santos," a man's voice boomed. "Look at you now. All caught up in your own web." The man had a thick accent, the kind my older uncles from Puerto Rico had when they tried really hard to speak English.

"Luca . . . I . . . I . . . can . . . ," Eduardo stuttered, his body trembling so hard it was making mine move. Now I could sense fear and anguish in Eduardo's voice. That was the first time Eduardo had sounded like he understood the seriousness of our situation.

"Shut up!" the man screamed. "You are a rat and in Mexico rats are killed and burned so that the dirty spirit does not corrupt anything around it."

I squeezed my eyes shut, but I couldn't keep the tears from bursting from the sides.

I was too afraid to even look at him. I kept my head down, but I had seen there were at least four more pairs of feet standing around. Eduardo and I had been working for this man and had never met him. I knew he was some big drug kingpin inside the Salazar Family Mexican drug cartel that operated out of Miami, but when I was making the money, I never thought of meeting him, especially not under these circumstances. I was helping this bastard get rich and couldn't even pick him out of a police lineup if my life depended on it.

"Please, Luca. I'm telling you I wasn't the rat. Maybe it was Lance . . . I mean, I just worked for him. He was the one responsible to you. He was the one who kept increasing everything. I did everything I could to keep this from happening," Eduardo pleaded his case, his words rushing out of his mouth.

"Oh, now you blame another man? Another cowardly move. Eduardo, I have people inside of the DEA who work for me. I know everything. If I didn't pay off the judge to set bail so I could get you and your little girlfriend out of there, you were prepared to sign a deal. You were prepared to tell everything. Like the fucking cocksucking rat that you are. You know nothing about death before dishonor. You would've sold out your own mother to get out of there. You failed the fucking test, you piece of shit," Luca spat, sucking his teeth. "Get him up," Luca said calmly, apparently unmoved by Eduardo's pleas.

"Luca! Luca! Give me another chance, please!" Eduardo begged, his voice coming out as a shrill scream.

His words exploded like bombs in my ears.

Another chance? Did that mean that Eduardo had snitched? Did that mean he put me in danger when I was only doing everything he ever told me to do? Did Eduardo sign my death sentence without even telling me what the fuck he was going to do? I immediately thought about my family again. These people obviously knew where I lived and where they could find my mother and my son. A wave of cramps trampled through my guts. Before I could control it, vomit spewed from my lips like lava from a volcano.

"What did you do to me, Eduardo?" I coughed and screamed through tears and vomit. I couldn't help it. I didn't care anymore. They were going to kill me anyway, right? "You fucking snitch! What did you do?" I gurgled. I had exercised more loyalty than Eduardo had. The men who were here to kill us said nothing and neither did Eduardo. I felt like someone had kicked me in the chest and the head right then. My heart was broken.

Two of Luca's goons cut the ropes that had kept Eduardo and I bound together. It was like they had cut the strings to my heart too. Eduardo didn't even look at me as they dragged him away screaming. I fell over onto my side, too weak to sit up on my own. Eduardo had betrayed me in the worst way. I was just a pawn in a much, much bigger game. And all for what? A few extra dollars a week that I didn't have anything to show for now except maybe some expensive pocketbooks, a few watches, some shoes, and an apartment I was surely going to never see again. Yes, I had been living ghetto fabulous, shopping for expensive things that I could've never imagined in my wildest dreams, but I had lost every dollar that I had ever stashed away for my son as "just in case" money. I had done all of this for him, and in the end I had left him nothing.

"Please. Please don't kill me," I begged through a waterfall of tears as I curled into a fetal position. With renewed spirit to see my son, I begged and pleaded for my life. I told them I wasn't a snitch and that I had no idea what Eduardo had done. I got nothing in response. There was a lot of Spanish being spoken, but I could only understand a fraction of it; so much for listening to my mother when she tried speaking Spanish to me all of my life.

"I promise I didn't speak to any DEA agents or the police. Please tell Luca that it wasn't me," I cried some more, pleading with the men who were left there to guard me. None of the remaining men acted like they could hear me. In my assessment, this was it. I was staring down a true death sentence. I immediately began praying. If my mother, a devout Catholic, had taught me nothing else, she had definitely taught me how to pray.

"Hail Mary full of Grace . . . ," I mumbled,

closing my eyes and preparing for my impending death. As soon as I closed my eyes, I was thrust backward in my mind, reviewing how I'd ever let the gorgeous, smooth-talking Eduardo Santos get my gullible ass into this mess.

If you enjoyed *Wife Extraordinaire Returns*, don't miss

Boss Divas

The most lethal ride-or-die women in Memphis now run their gangs and the streets. But the aftermath of an all-out war means merciless new enemies, time-bomb secrets . . . and one chance to take it all . . .

Available now wherever books and ebooks are sold.

1

Ta'Shara

"STOP THE FUCKING CAR!"

Profit slams on the brakes while I bolt out of the passenger car door and race into the night toward my foster parents' burning house.

"TRACEE! REGGIE!" *They're not in there. Please, God. Don't let them be in there.* "TRACEE! REGGIE!"

"Ta'Shara, wait up," Profit yells. His long strides eat up the distance between us even as I shove my way through the city's emergency responders. I've never seen flames stretch so high or felt such intense heat. Still, none of that shit stops me. In my delusional mind, there is still time to get them out of there.

"Hey, lady. You can't go in there," someone shouts, and makes a grab for me.

As I draw closer to the front porch, Profit is able to wrap one of his powerful arms around my waist and lift me off my feet. "Baby, stop. You can't go in there."

"Let me go!" My legs pedal in the air as I stretch uselessly for the door. "TRACEE! REGGIE!" My screams rake my throat raw.

Profit drags me away from the growing flames.

Men in uniform rush over to us. I don't know who they are and I don't care. I just need to know one thing. "Where are my parents? Did they make it out?"

"Ma'am, calm down. Please tell me your name."

"WHERE ARE THEY?"

"Ma'am—"

"ANSWER ME, DAMMIT!"

"C'mon, man," Profit says. "Give my girl something."

The fireman draws a deep breath and then drops a bomb that changes my life forever.

"The neighbors reported the fire. Right now, I'm not aware of anyone making it out of the house. I'm sorry."

"NOOOOOOO!" I collapse in Profit's arms. He hauls me up against his six-three frame, and I lay my head on his broad chest. Before, I found comfort in his strong embrace, but not tonight. I sob uncontrollably as pain overwhelms me, but then I make out a familiar car down the street.

"Oh. My. God."

Profit tenses. "What?"

My eyes aren't deceiving me. Sitting behind the wheel of her burgundy Crown Victoria is LeShelle with a slow smile creeping across her face. She forms a gun with her hand and pretends to fire at us.

We're next.

LeShelle tosses back her head, and despite the siren's wail, the roaring fire, and the chaos around me, that bitch's maniacal laugh rings in my ears.

How much more of this shit am I going to take? When will this fuckin' bullshit end?

BOOM!

The crowd gasps while windows explode from the top floor of the house, but my gaze never waivers from LeShelle. My tears dry up as anger grips me.

She did this shit. I don't need a jury to tell me that the bitch is guilty as hell. How long has she been threatening the Douglas's lives? Why in the hell didn't I believe that she would follow through?

LeShelle has proven her ruthlessness time after time. This fucking Gangster Disciples versus the Vice Lords shit ain't a game to her. It's a way of life. And she doesn't give a fuck who she hurts.

My blood boils and all at once everything bursts out of me. I wrench away from Profit's protective arms and take off toward LeShelle in a rage.

"I'M GOING TO FUCKING KILL YOU!"

"TA'SHARA, NO," Profit shouts.

I ignore him as I race toward LeShelle's car. My hot tears burn tracks down my face.

LeShelle laughs in my face and then pulls off from the curb, but not before I'm able to pound my fist against the trunk.

Profit's arms wrap back around my waist, but I kick out and connect with LeShelle's taillight and shatter that mutherfucka. The small wave of satisfaction I get is quickly erased when her piece of shit car burps out a black cloud of exhaust in my face.

"NO! Don't let her get away. No!"

"Ta'Shara, please. Not now. Let it go!"

Let it go? I round on Profit. "How the fuck can you say that shit?"

BOOM!

More windows explode, drawing my attention back to the only place that I've ever called home. My heart claws its way out of my chest as orange flames and black smoke lick the sky.

My legs give out and my knees kiss the concrete; all the while, Profit's arms remain locked around me. I can't hear what he's saying because my sobs drown him out.

"This is all my fault," tumbles over my tongue. I conjure up an image of Tracee and Reggie: the last time I'd seen them. It's a horrible memory. Everyone was angry and everyone said things that can never be taken back.

Grief consumes me. I squeeze my eyes tight and cling to the ghosts inside of my head. "I'm sorry. I'm so sorry."

Profit's arms tighten. I melt in his arms even though I want to lash out. *Isn't it his fault for my foster parents roasting in that house too?* When the question crosses my mind, I crumble from the weight of my shame.

I'm to blame. No one else.

A heap in the center of the street, I lay my head against Profit's chest again and take in the horrific sight through a steady sheen of tears. The Douglases were good people. All they wanted was the best for me and for me to believe in myself. They would've done the same for LeShelle if she'd given them the chance.

LeShelle fell in love with the streets and the make-believe power of being the head bitch of the Queen Gs. I didn't want anything to do with any of that bullshit, but it didn't matter. I'm viewed as GD property by blood, and the shit hit the fan when I fell in love with Profit—a Vice Lord by blood. Back then Profit wasn't a soldier yet. But our being together was taken as a sign of disrespect. LeShelle couldn't let it slide.

However, the harder I fight the street's politics, the deeper I'm dragged into her bullshit world of gangs and violence.

"I should have killed her when I had the chance." If I had, Tracee and Reggie would still be alive. "She won't get away with this," I vow. "I'm going to kill her if it's the last thing I do."

Grab the Hottest Fiction
from
Dafina Books